KU-437-993

The Thorn Birds

COLLEEN McCULLOUGH

Level 6

Retold by Ann Ward
Series Editor: Derek Strange

PENGUIN BOOKS

PENGUIN BOOKS

Published by the Penguin Group
Penguin Books Ltd, 27 Wrights Lane, London W8 5TZ
Penguin Books USA Inc., 375 Hudson Street, New York, New York 10014, USA
Penguin Books Australia Ltd, Ringwood, Victoria, Australia
Penguin Books Canada Ltd, 10 Alcorn Avenue, Toronto, Ontario, Canada M4V 3B2
Penguin Books (NZ) Ltd, 182–190 Wairau Road, Auckland 10, New Zealand

Penguin Books Ltd, Registered Offices: Harmondsworth, Middlesex, England

Copyright © Colleen McCullough 1977
First published by HarperCollins Publishers
This adaptation published by Penguin Books 1995
10 9 8 7 6 5 4 3

Copyright © Ann Ward 1995
Illustrations copyright © David Cuzik 1995
All rights reserved

The moral right of the adapter and of the illustrator has been asserted

Illustrations by David Cuzik

Filmset by Datix International Limited, Bungay, Suffolk
Printed in England by Clays Ltd, St Ives plc
Set in 11/14pt Monophoto Bembo

Except in the United States of America, this book is sold subject
to the condition that it shall not, by way of trade or otherwise, be lent,
resold, hired out, or otherwise circulated without the publisher's
prior consent in any form of binding or cover other than that in
which it is published and without a similar condition including this
condition being imposed on the subsequent purchaser

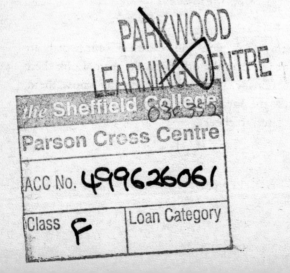

PARKWOOD
LEARNING CENTRE
the Sheffield College
Parson Cross Centre
ACC No. 4996260061
Class F   Loan Category

'Meggie, I want you to forget me,' Father Ralph said. 'I want you to look around and find a good, kind man, marry him, have babies. You'll be a good mother. I can never leave the Church, and I don't love you the way a husband will. Forget me, Meggie!'

There is a legend about a bird that sings only once. From the time it is born, it searches for a thorn tree and, when it finds one, it flies at the longest, sharpest thorn. As it dies, it sings its song – more beautiful than that of any other bird.

In Australia, in the early years of this century, Meggie Cleary is searching for a way to sing *her* song. She is strong and beautiful but she loves only one man, a man it is impossible to love – the kind, handsome priest, Father Ralph de Bricassart. Can she ever win him? Is it right to win him? Or can she forget him, and love someone else?

The story of her struggle is the story of her whole life – a life of pain, happiness, tragedy and simple, hard living in an untamed land. From the farms of New South Wales to the sugar cane fields of Queensland, Australia asks a lot of its people. But the best is only bought with great pain. Or so the legend says . . .

The Thorn Birds is one of the biggest-selling, most widely read novels ever written. It sold nine million copies in its first four years in the United States alone. A mini-series for television, starring Richard Chamberlain and Rachel Ward, was made in 1983, and won even more readers for the novel.

Colleen McCullough was born in 1937 in Wellington, New South Wales, in Australia. Her father was an Irishman who went to live in Australia in the 1920s and her mother was from New Zealand. The story of *The Thorn Birds* is partly taken from her own family history.

Ms McCullough lived alone for some years but now lives with her husband on Norfolk Island in the South Pacific.

To the teacher:

In addition to all the language forms of Levels One to Five, which are used again at this level of the series, the main verb forms and tenses used at Level Six are:

- future perfect verbs, passives with continuous or perfect aspects and the 'third' conditional with continuous forms
- modal verbs: *needn't* and *needn't have* (to express absence of necessity), *would* (to describe habitual past actions), *should* and *should have* (to express probability or failed expectation), *may have* and *might have* (to express possibility), *could have* and *would have* (to express past, unfulfilled possibility or likelihood).

Also used are:

- non-defining relative clauses.

Specific attention is paid to vocabulary development in the Vocabulary Work exercises at the end of the book. These exercises are aimed at training students to enlarge their vocabulary systematically through intelligent reading and effective use of a dictionary.

To the student:

Dictionary Words:

- As you read this book, you will find that some words are in darker black ink than the others on the page. Look them up in your dictionary, if you do not already know them, or try to guess the meaning of the words first, and then look them up later, to check.

Chapter One

On 8 December 1915, Meggie Cleary had her fourth birthday. After breakfast her mother gave her something wrapped in brown paper and told her to go outside and open it. Meggie sat down beside the front gate, her small fingers struggling with the heavy paper, which smelled of the Wahine general store.

At 'last she saw something gold and shiny. Her fingers moved faster and there at last was her birthday present.

'Agnes! Oh, Agnes!' she said softly, as she stared at the **doll**.

Meggie had seen the doll months ago in the general store on her only visit to Wahine, the nearest village to their home in New Zealand. She had given it the name Agnes then, and she had often thought about it. But she never dreamt it would be hers some day.

The doll had golden hair and a pink dress. She held it and looked at it without moving. She was still sitting there when her brothers Jack and Hughie came quietly up behind her.

'What's that you've got, Meggie?' Jack shouted. 'Show us!'

'Yes, show us!' Hughie laughed.

Meggie held the doll tighter and shook her head. 'No, she's mine. I got her for my birthday!'

'Go on! We just want to look.'

She held up the doll so that her brothers could see. 'Look, isn't she beautiful? Her name's Agnes.'

Hughie looked at the doll and whistled. 'Hey, Jack, look! It can move its hand!'

'Where? Let's see.'

'No!' Meggie held her doll close again. There were tears in

1

her eyes. 'No, you'll break her! Don't take her away – you'll break her!'

But Jack's dirty brown hands grabbed Meggie's wrists, and Hughie tried to pull the doll away from her.

Meggie's tears were running down her face now. 'Don't take her, please!' she cried. She held the doll and tried to kick the boys.

'Got it!' Hughie shouted as he pulled the doll away from Meggie.

Jack and Hughie found the doll very interesting. They took off the dress and pushed and pulled at the doll's arms and legs. They turned her head round and bent her legs back. They forgot about Meggie, standing beside them, crying.

One of the boys stood on the doll's dress as it lay on the ground. His boots were muddy. Meggie knelt on the ground, her eyes full of tears, and tried to find the doll's clothes in the long grass.

◆

Frank was working in the **barn**, making shoes for horses. He had started work six months before, and he hated it. He was sixteen years old, small and thin, but strong. All the other Cleary children had red hair, but Frank's hair was black. He stopped work, put on his shirt and left the barn.

The Clearys' house was on top of a hill. Like all New Zealand houses, it was made of wood. Around it stretched the green grass, dotted with thousands of sheep.

Frank hurried towards the house. Then he saw Meggie and the boys. Meggie's dress was dirty and she was still trying to stop her brothers playing with her doll.

Frank shouted and Jack and Hughie ran, dropping the doll. They were afraid of Frank's anger.

'Don't let me catch you touching that doll again!' he shouted after them. Then he turned gently to Meggie.

'Got it!' Hughie shouted as he pulled the doll away from Meggie.

'There's no need to cry! Come on now, give me a smile for your birthday.'

Meggie's grey eyes were large and full of sadness. Frank wiped her tearful face with a dirty handkerchief. Meggie picked up her doll and began to comb the golden hair. Then a terrible thing happened. All Agnes's hair came off, and all Meggie could see was an empty hole and the inside of the doll's head. Meggie screamed in fright and threw the doll away.

Frank picked up his little sister and held her in his arms. He could not imagine why she was so frightened.

It was half an hour before Meggie would look at the doll again. Frank spoke to her gently. 'Come on now, it's time to go inside. We'll ask Mum to help us to mend Agnes, eh?'

Fiona Cleary was in the kitchen, preparing the meal. She was very handsome, but she rarely smiled. Although she had six children, she still had a good figure. She spent her days in the kitchen and the back garden, cooking, washing and gardening.

She turned to look at Meggie and Frank.

'Meggie, look at you. Your best dress is dirty!'

'It isn't her fault, Mum,' said Frank. 'Jack and Hughie took her doll away. I said we'd mend it. Can we?'

'Let me see.'

Fee was a silent woman. Nobody knew what she was thinking. She finished looking at the doll, and put it on top of the cupboard near the stove.

'I'll wash her clothes tomorrow morning, and do her hair again. Frank can stick her hair back on after tea tonight.'

Meggie nodded. She wished her mother would sometimes smile. Frank knew that Fee didn't smile much because she was always tired. There was so much to do with six children and little money.

♦

Padraic Cleary was often away from home, working, but he was at home for Meggie's birthday. When he came home in the evening the younger boys were playing outside and Frank was cutting wood.

'Go and help Frank,' he told Jack and Bob. Then he went into the kitchen and nodded to Fiona. He sat down in the only comfortable chair in the kitchen. Meggie came to him and sat on his knee.

He leaned back in his chair. 'How does it feel to be four, Meggie?' he asked his daughter.

'It feels good, Daddy.'

'Did Mum give you your present?'

'Oh, Daddy, how did you and Mum know I wanted Agnes? She's beautiful! I want to look at her all day!'

'She's lucky to have anything to look at,' said Fee. 'Jack and Hughie got hold of the doll.'

'Is it badly damaged?'

'It can be mended. Frank caught the boys before they could do too much damage.'

'Frank? Why wasn't he working? He's got too much work to do to come up here during the day.'

'He just came up for a tool,' Fee said quickly. She thought Padraic was too hard on Frank.

Padraic Cleary was a small man with thick red hair. He had come from Ireland to the Southern Hemisphere twenty years before, and he still spoke like an Irishman. Although he had to work very hard for very little money, he was a happy man.

Fiona went to the back door and shouted, 'Dinner!'

The boys came into the kitchen one by one. The last was Frank, carrying wood for the fire. The family sat down around the big old table in the kitchen, and Fiona served the meat, boiled potatoes and beans.

After the meal the family drank cups of tea, read or talked.

Meggie and the two younger boys, Stu and Hughie, went to bed, Jack and Bob went outside to feed the dogs and Frank took Meggie's doll and began to stick its hair back on. Padraic closed his book and stood up.

'Well, I'm off to bed.'

'Good night, Paddy.'

Fee began to wash the dishes. Frank waited until his father went upstairs and then helped his mother. Padraic did not like to see the boys helping their mother. That was women's work.

'I wish you had servants to help you,' said Frank. 'You work too hard.'

'Don't talk like that, Frank,' said his mother. 'Your father is a good man, and he does his best for us.'

Fee looked at Frank as he worked. She wished Frank was not so unhappy at home. She wished he and Paddy would not argue so often.

'Good night, Frank, and thank you,' she said.

Chapter Two

After the summer holidays, Meggie started school in the village. On her first morning, Meggie and her brothers were late. The first person Meggie saw outside the school was the teacher, Sister Agatha. Meggie stared at her black clothes and her severe, unsmiling face. The boys knew that they would be punished for their lateness and waited silently.

'Well, Robert Cleary. Why are you late?' Sister Agatha shouted at Bob.

'I'm sorry, Sister.'

Meggie was frightened, but she spoke. 'Oh, please, Sister, it was my fault.'

Sister Agatha's cold blue eyes looked at the little girl.

'Why was it your fault?' she asked coldly.

'I was sick. Mum had to change my clothes,' said Meggie.

'Silence!' said Sister Agatha. 'I don't care if it was your fault. You are all late and you will all be punished. Six cuts.'

Meggie watched as her brothers held out their hands and Sister Agatha's stick rose and fell. Then it was her turn. The pain was terrible, but she was too proud and too angry to cry. She sat at her desk, too hurt and frightened to understand what was happening or to look at the other children.

And so Meggie's schooldays began. She was a clever child, but she was too frightened of Sister Agatha to learn very much. Meggie started to write with her left hand, and Sister Agatha put the pencil into her right, and tied her left hand behind her back with rope. This happened every day for two months.

♦

Two days before Christmas in 1917, Paddy brought home a newspaper with pictures of the war in Europe. They showed soldiers from Australia and New Zealand fighting bravely. Frank read the paper eagerly, his eyes shining.

'Daddy, I want to go!' he said, as he lay the paper down on the table.

Fee turned round quickly and Paddy put down his book.

'You're too young, Frank,' he said.

'No, I'm not! I'm seventeen, Daddy, I'm a man!'

'You're too young, Frank, they won't take you.'

'If you say I can go, they'll take me.'

'But I don't want you to go. We need the money you earn.'

'Let me go, please. I'll be paid and it's my only chance to do better.'

'Nonsense, boy. You don't know what you're talking about. War is terrible. You're not big enough to be a soldier.'

Frank's face turned red. He was not very tall, but he was

strong. He was often involved in fights with the local young men, trying to prove that he was the strongest.

Later that evening, Meggie climbed out of her bedroom window and found Frank sitting on his own outside the house.

'You're not really going away are you, Frank?' she asked him. 'We need you here.'

'I've done so much for the family,' said Frank, sadly, 'Now I must try to do something for myself. When you're older, you'll understand. Now, Meggie, you mustn't tell anybody about our talk.'

'I won't tell.'

'Good. Now go to bed.'

In the morning Frank was gone. When Meggie came down for breakfast, the boys were sitting silently and Paddy's chair was empty.

'Where's Daddy?' Meggie asked.

'He's gone to ask the police to bring Frank back,' said Fee. 'Poor Frank!' she sighed.

The police brought Frank back three days later. From that day Paddy hardly spoke to Frank.

TWO:
1921–1928 RALPH

Chapter Three

Father Ralph de Bricassart drove his new car along the road from Gillanbone to Drogheda. At last he saw the house. Drogheda was the biggest property in the district, and the house, too, was the largest and finest. It was surrounded by gardens, with green grass and roses and large shady trees. Behind the house there were many farm buildings and the houses for the workers on the property.

Father Ralph got out of his car and walked to the front door. Inside the house Mary Carson was waiting for him, sitting in her big old chair by the window. Her hair was still bright red, and her face looked young for a woman of sixty-five. Her blue eyes were hard.

'Will you have tea, Father?' she asked. Her face softened as she looked at the priest. 'And may I ask you some questions?'

Father Ralph thought of her gift of a new car. He did not like having to feel grateful, but Mrs Carson was indeed very generous. He nodded.

'How old are you?' she asked.

'Twenty-eight.'

'They don't usually send priests like you to a little town like Gillanbone. What did you do?'

'I insulted the **bishop**,' he said, smiling.

'That was foolish,' she said. 'I suppose you want to be powerful in the Church. That won't happen if you stay here.'

'Yes, but I have you. And I can visit Drogheda.'

She was pleased to have him there. She enjoyed his beauty and his attractiveness, his curly black hair and blue eyes. He must know that he was handsome.

Mary Carson's husband had died thirty-three years before, and she had no children. Nobody in the district found it strange that she enjoyed being with the handsome young priest; he was popular with everybody, rich and poor.

As they were eating their tea Mary Carson sighed. 'Dear Father, I want you to pray for me.'

'I always pray for you.'

'I'm looking for a man to manage the farm.'

'Again? How many managers have you had in the past year?'

'Five. It's hard to find the right man for the job.' She looked at the priest thoughtfully. 'You think I haven't any family. Do you think I'm going to die and leave all my money and my land to the Church?'

'I have no idea,' he said carelessly.

'In fact, I have a brother with a large family of sons.'

'That's nice for you.'

'I was a poor country girl when I came from Ireland to Australia but I married a rich man.'

'And your brother?' he asked.

'He's eleven years younger than I am. I hardly know him. He lives in New Zealand now. He hasn't made any money there. Last night when the manager left here, I suddenly thought of Padraic. He knows the land, he understands farming and sheep. I'm going to write and ask him to come here with his family. Then when I die he can have Drogheda.' As she spoke, she watched the priest carefully.

'It will be nice for you, hearing young voices around the house.'

'Oh, they won't live in the house with me. There's a manager's house at the back. They can live there.'

◆

Six days before Meggie's ninth birthday, her brother Harold was born. The family were having a hard time; there was not much work for Paddy and the boys, and the baby was not strong.

Then one day Paddy received a letter from Mary Carson. The family watched anxiously as he opened it. Paddy looked up, excited.

'We're going to Australia!' he shouted.

Fee read the letter. 'Is she going to send us the money to get to Australia?' she asked.

'We can manage,' said Paddy proudly. 'We've got enough money for that.'

So Paddy arranged for them to take a ship to Australia at the end of August.

◆

The voyage from New Zealand to Australia took three days. The sea was rough and they were all seasick. The family had only a tiny room on the ship, which smelled of oil. Fee was so ill they thought she would die.

As the ship approached Sydney, the sea became calm and the weather became cold and foggy. Paddy carried Fee off the ship in his arms. They found a taxi which would take the whole family and drove into the city. The children had never seen such a big town.

Fee rested in a hotel room while Paddy went out to find out about a train to Gillanbone.

'Do you think you could manage the journey tonight?' Paddy asked Fee when he returned. 'If we don't go tonight, it's a week until the next train to Gillanbone.'

'I think Mum should rest,' said Frank.

'You don't understand, Frank,' said Paddy. 'We don't have enough money to stay for a whole week in Sydney.'

'I'll manage, Paddy,' said Fee.

'How far is it, Daddy?' asked Meggie as they settled down on the train.

'Six hundred and ten miles,' said Paddy. 'We'll be there late tomorrow afternoon.'

The train travelled through the night, and Meggie slept. In the morning they looked out at the Australian countryside. Instead of the green New Zealand hills, everything was brown and grey, even the trees. Fee looked at it without changing her expression, but Meggie's eyes filled with tears. It was horrible!

It had been freezing cold at night in the train, but now, as the sun rose in the sky, it became hotter and hotter. They felt uncomfortable in their heavy winter clothing, even with the train windows open. As the sun went down, they arrived at Gillanbone, a small town of wooden and iron buildings on either side of a broad, dusty street.

A shining black car was standing outside the station, and a tall young priest came towards them, the red dust rising around his feet.

'Hello, I'm Father de Bricassart,' he said. 'You must be Mary's brother.' He looked round at the family. Meggie stood behind the boys, looking up at him with her mouth open. He bent down and held her. 'Well! And who are you?' he asked her, smiling.

'Meggie,' she said.

'My favourite name,' he said, and stood up. 'It will be better for you all to stay with me in town tonight. I'll drive you to Drogheda in the morning.'

When his guests had gone to bed, Father Ralph thought about them. Paddy was like Mary Carson, Fee was tired but beautiful, the boys, except for Frank, were like their father, but Meggie was the most beautiful child he had ever seen, with red-gold hair and clear grey eyes which shone like silver.

In the morning he drove the family to Drogheda. 'Are we going to live *here*?' asked Meggie as they approached the great stone house.

'Not exactly,' said the priest quickly. 'Your house is beside the river, behind the big house.'

Mary Carson did not rise from her chair when her brother and his family came in. 'Well, Paddy,' she said to her brother. She did not greet Fee and the children. 'You must be anxious to get home, Father,' she said to the priest.

Father Ralph was carrying Meggie in his arms. 'Not at all,' he said. 'I've promised Meggie to show her her new home.'

'Meggie?' said Mary Carson.

'Yes, this is Meggie,' said Father Ralph, and introduced the whole family. Mary Carson hardly listened, she was staring at the priest with Meggie in his arms.

Chapter Four

Gradually the family began to settle down in their new home. The Drogheda lands were enormous, and the nearest small town, Gillanbone, was forty miles away. Paddy and the boys loved the life. They often spent days away from home, riding their horses and sleeping under the stars.

Although it was still early spring, the weather was hot. Then in the middle of January, black rainclouds appeared. Paddy and the boys worked long hours, moving the sheep away from the river onto higher ground. Father Ralph came to help. He rode a horse that Mary Carson had given him, as he went with Frank and the dogs to move the sheep from the banks of the river. Frank looked at the priest and envied him his beautiful horse and his expensive clothes. Of all the boys, Frank was the least happy at Drogheda. He wanted to leave and go to Sydney. On the evening of the second day, when Frank and Father Ralph had managed to move all the sheep, the rains fell. Within minutes the ground was a sea of mud, and as they approached the river they had to get down from their horses. When they got to the river the horses were able to cross but the men couldn't; it was too deep and too fast. At last Paddy came with a rope and pulled them across.

'I'll change my clothes at the big house,' said Father Ralph.

Mary Carson watched him as he dried himself and thought again that he was the most beautiful man she had ever seen. 'Do you need women, Ralph?' she asked.

'No!' he said.

Mary sat in her chair and wished that she was a younger woman. When at last the rain stopped and Father Ralph returned to Gillanbone, he had a cheque for one thousand pounds in his pocket. The bishop would be pleased with him.

At the beginning of February Meggie and Stuart started school in Gillanbone. It was different from their school in New Zealand. Here the teachers were kind to them, it was quiet and peaceful, and nobody ever shouted at them. Father Ralph visited them at school often, and they often stayed with him at his house. He had Meggie's room painted pale green, and bought new curtains for it.

In the meantime, work at Drogheda continued. Frank had been working away from home for two weeks. When he returned he noticed that his mother was again expecting a baby.

'Oh, God!' he said angrily. 'He has no right! He should have left you alone!'

'Don't talk like that, Frank,' said his mother.

Frank turned and left the room.

Chapter Five

When winter came it was time for the Gillanbone **Show**. Fee wasn't well enough to go, so Paddy drove Mary Carson into town in her car.

Paddy offered to buy Frank a drink in a bar, but Frank refused and went off on his own. He went to the priest's house and found Meggie.

'Come on, Meggie, I'll take you to the show,' he said, holding out his hand.

'Why don't I take you both?' Father Ralph asked.

Meggie, with the two men she loved most, was in heaven. The show was wonderful, with lots of things to see and do. The biggest tent was occupied by Jimmy Sharman's boxing show. Eight boxers were standing outside. 'Come on, boys, who'll take a glove?' a big man shouted. 'Who wants a go? Take a glove, win five pounds!'

'Come on, boys, who'll take a glove?' a big man shouted.
'Who wants a go?'

'I will!' Frank shouted. 'I will! I will!' He pushed himself to the front of the crowd. Some of the crowd laughed because Frank was so small. Father Ralph wanted to stay and see what happened, but he thought it would be better to take Meggie away. But Meggie began to scream, and people turned to look at her.

'I want to stay with Frank!' she screamed. So the priest got out his money and they followed the crowd into the tent. He found a place near the back, and held on to Meggie tightly.

Frank was the first one to fight. It was unusual for someone from the crowd to beat one of Jimmy Sharman's boxers, but Frank knocked the first boxer down and offered to fight another. The crowd became excited and more and more people crowded into the tent. By the time Frank was finished he had fought four men and he had won twenty pounds.

Meggie rushed out of the tent, feeling sick. She started to cry, and Father Ralph gave her his handkerchief.

Frank came out of the tent, his lip bleeding. He looked happy for the first time since Father Ralph had met him.

◆

Paddy's day with his sister had not been easy. So when he got back to Father Ralph's house and found Frank, Meggie and Father Ralph resting beside the fire and drinking tea, he felt angry. He looked at Frank's bleeding lip.

'What will your mother think?' he shouted. 'You've been fighting again!'

Father Ralph started to explain, but Frank jumped up and waved the twenty pound notes in Paddy's face.

'I knocked out four boxers. I earned all this money in a few minutes! You might not like it, but everybody else thinks I'm great!'

'Oh, grow up, Frank.'

Frank's face turned white. 'Jimmy Sharman says I've got a

great future as a boxer. He wants to train me and he wants to pay me! I can knock down any man, including you. I'll teach you to leave my mother alone!'

'No! no! no!' Meggie screamed. Father Ralph held her shoulders tightly. Tears ran down her face. 'No, Daddy, no! Oh, Frank, please! Please, please!' she screamed.

But only Father Ralph heard her. Frank and Paddy faced each other angrily.

'I'm your mother's husband,' said Paddy, trying to be calm.

'You're no better than a dog,' shouted Frank.

'And you're no better than your father, whoever he was. Thank God I'm not your father!' shouted Paddy. Then he stopped and his anger left him. 'I didn't mean it. I didn't mean it,' he said.

Father Ralph let go of Meggie and seized Frank. Meggie sank to the floor, her eyes full of tears, looking first at her father then at Frank. She didn't understand what was happening but she knew it was something terribly serious.

'You meant it,' said Frank softly. 'And I think I've always known it. Let me go, Father. I won't touch him.'

Father Ralph was angry. 'Look what you've done to this child, both of you! I couldn't take her away. I was afraid you'd kill each other.'

'It's all right. I'm going,' Frank said. 'I'm going to join Jim Sharman's show and I won't be back.'

'You've got to come back,' Paddy whispered. 'What will I tell your mother? You know how much she loves you.'

'Tell her I'm going because I want to be someone. It's true.'

Frank picked up his hat and coat and walked to the door.

Paddy stared with shocked eyes at Meggie, who was extremely upset. He got up to go to her, but Father Ralph pushed him away.

'Leave her alone. You've done enough! I'm going to put the child to bed. Then I'll come back and talk to you.'

Father Ralph took Meggie to her room and put her to bed. He talked gently to her as he did so, but he didn't know if she heard him. Her eyes were full of pain.

'Is she all right?' asked Paddy as the priest came back into the room.

Father Ralph poured himself a drink.

'I don't know. Paddy, why did you get so angry? Why did you say those things to Frank? It's true, of course. I realized Frank wasn't your son. He's got black hair, and all the others have red hair, like you. Why don't you tell me about it?'

Paddy stared at the fire, then he began to speak.

'I don't know who Frank's father is. Frank was born before I met Fee. When I arrived in New Zealand, I went to work for a very rich family, one of the wealthiest in the country. Fee was the only daughter.

'I never spoke to her, but sometimes I'd see this beautiful young lady walking with a little boy. Except for her grandmother, all her family were ashamed of her – she had a child and she wasn't married. When her grandmother died, her father came to me and offered to pay me five hundred pounds if I would marry her and take her far away.

'Well, Father, it was a lot of money. I wanted to get married, but I didn't know any girls in New Zealand. So I accepted the offer. I spoke to Fee for the first time on the day that I married her. At first I was frightened of her, she was so strange and so beautiful.'

'She's still beautiful, Paddy,' said Father Ralph gently.

'We've had a hard life, Father, but she's been safe with me. I love her very much, but she loves only Frank. Now I've sent Frank away, and she'll never forgive me.'

'Don't tell her about the fight, Paddy. Just say that Frank went away with the boxers.'

'I couldn't do that, Father,' said Paddy, shocked. 'And what about Meggie? She heard everything.'

18

'Don't worry about Meggie, I'll talk to her. I don't think she understood what you said.'

Meggie wasn't asleep. The priest sat down beside her.

'Frank has gone away, Meggie,' he said.

'I know, Father. I'm going to go with him. He needs me.'

'You can't, my Meggie. You see, Frank's got his own life, and it's time he went away. He's wanted to go for a long time. Do you understand that, Meggie?'

Her eyes, which were tired and full of pain, moved to his face. 'I know,' she said. 'I know. Will I ever see him again?'

'I don't know,' said Father Ralph.

Chapter Six

It was August, and very cold. Fee wasn't well, and she needed Meggie at home to help her. Stuart didn't want to stay at school without Meggie, so he came home too.

Fee felt too tired to look after little Hal, so Meggie became like a mother to him. It was hard work for the girl, but she was happy. Nobody mentioned Frank. Fee waited for a letter from him, but it never came.

Then the twins were born, two little boys, James and Patrick. Fee felt too ill and tired to look after them, but the servants from the big house loved Jims and Patsy, as they were called. Soon the twins were spending most of their time at the big house.

◆

Father Ralph watched Meggie as she brushed Patsy's red hair. Then he turned and stared towards the big house, hidden behind the trees. What was the old spider, Mary Carson, planning?

'What are you thinking, Father?' asked Meggie.

'Er . . . nothing. Let's go and see your Auntie Mary, shall we?' They walked together up the path to the big house.

As Father Ralph came in, holding Meggie's hand, Mary Carson stared at Meggie coldly.

'Go to the kitchen, girl. Have your tea with Mrs Smith,' said Mary sharply.

'Why don't you like Meggie?' Father Ralph asked as he sat down.

'Because you do,' she answered.

'Oh, come now, Mary!' he said. 'She's just a little girl.'

She laughed. 'You've changed, Ralph,' she said. 'You're less ambitious than you were once. Don't you want to be a **cardinal**?'

He looked unhappy. 'It's impossible now!'

'We'll see,' she laughed unpleasantly. 'I know what you really want, Ralph. Maybe I will help you to get what you want in the end. But I'll make sure it hurts you. I'll make sure you suffer for it.'

◆

The sky filled with clouds and Paddy began to hope for rain.

'Dry storms,' said Mary Carson. 'We won't get any rain for a long time.'

The grass began to get thin and the wind blew clouds of dust across the brown fields. One day little Hal started to cough, and his health quickly got worse. At first Fee wasn't worried, but by the time Paddy came home, the child's lips were blue, and he couldn't breathe.

Paddy telephoned the doctor, forty miles away, but the doctor couldn't come. Meggie held her little brother and prayed. She was frightened because there was nothing she could do. Then Paddy and Fee started to pray. At last, at midnight, Paddy lifted the child from Meggie's arms and laid him on the bed.

Meggie was half asleep, but her eyes suddenly opened wide. 'Oh, Daddy, he's better!' she said.

But Paddy only shook his head. 'No, Meggie, but he's at peace. He's gone to God.'

'Daddy means he's dead,' said Fee.

'Oh, Daddy, no! He can't be dead!'

But Meggie knew that her little brother was dead. He looked like a doll, not a child.

Father Ralph found Meggie sitting on her own when he came in with the doctor. He knew how much she loved her little brother, and as he watched her, sitting so patiently, he thought she looked older. Who had taught her to be so brave?

'Oh, Meggie,' he said helplessly.

She looked and him and gave him a smile of great love. As he looked into her eyes, he suddenly felt afraid for them both.

Chapter Seven

Mary Carson was planning a big party for her seventy-second birthday. Sitting in her usual chair, she gave orders for the garden to be tidied up and for the biggest room in the house to be made ready for the dancing. A band was coming from Sydney and special food was ordered.

While everybody was busy, Mary Carson took a big piece of paper and began to write. It was something she had planned to do for years. She finished writing, and then a laugh from outside the window made her suddenly angry.

Father Ralph was teaching Meggie to ride. He had bought her riding clothes in Gillanbone, and for a few hours every week gave her riding lessons. Meggie was growing up and, although she knew it was impossible, she often dreamed of what it would be like to be kissed by the priest.

As Mary Carson watched through the window, Father Ralph and Meggie walked past with their horses. Mary wished that she could stop the riding lessons, or ride with them herself. She hated their friendship, and she wondered why Paddy and Fee did not stop their daughter spending so much time with the priest.

Mary took another piece of paper and began to write again.

♦

Everybody had new clothes for the party. Meggie's dress was long, and pinkish grey. Her red curly hair was cut short. Paddy looked at her and realized that she wasn't a little girl any more. In a month, she would be seventeen.

It was a splendid party. Mary Carson's neighbours had come from many miles away; they knew how rich she was, and expected there would be wonderful food and wine.

Father Ralph didn't speak to Meggie during dinner or afterwards. He couldn't explain to her that everyone in the room was watching him. Most were watching her, too; she was the most beautiful woman there. He felt proud of her, but he also felt sorry that she was growing up.

At three o'clock in the morning Mary Carson stood up. 'I'm going to bed now,' she told her guests. 'But please don't stop dancing. Father Ralph, will you help me to go upstairs, please?'

But they didn't go upstairs. She unlocked a downstairs room and they went inside.

'It was a good party, Mary,' he said.

'My last. I'm tired of living and I want to stop.'

He felt tired, too. He had no real friends in Gillanbone. He was now thirty-five years old, and he wasn't going anywhere. He wouldn't become a powerful man in the Church now.

'I've often wanted to be younger, Ralph,' she said. 'If I was younger we'd be more than friends, you and I. I hate my life – and I think I'd like to destroy yours.'

He laughed, feeling uncomfortable. 'Oh, my dear Mary! I know that.'

'If I was younger we'd be more than friends, you and I.
I hate my life – and I think I'd like to destroy yours.'

'But do you know why? It's because I love you, and you don't love me. I want you, and I can't have you because I'm too old. But I'm not too old to have feelings.'

She stared at him for a long time, with a hard look in her eyes. Suddenly, he felt afraid of her.

'Ralph, there's an envelope in my desk. Will you bring it to me, please?'

He gave her the thick white envelope.

'It's yours,' she said, and laughed. 'I know exactly what you'll do when you open it. It'll change your life. I've lost you to Meggie, but she'll never have you.'

'Why do you hate Meggie?'

'Because you love her. But I don't want to talk about Meggie. I'll never see you again, and I don't want to waste time. Now promise that you won't open that envelope until I'm dead.'

'All right. I promise.'

'Goodbye then. I'll die tonight.'

He didn't believe her, but he didn't want to argue.

♦

Outside it was still dark, and inside the big house the party continued noisily. Father Ralph walked through the garden, wanting to get far away from Mary Carson and her plans. He felt alone in the world. Then he heard someone crying in the darkness. It was Meggie and he knew he must go to her.

'Darling Meggie, don't cry,' he said, sitting down beside her on the grass. 'How long have you been sitting out here?'

'Since midnight. I told the others I was going to bed.'

'What's the matter, Meggie?'

'You didn't speak to me tonight!'

'I thought that was it. Meggie, you were the prettiest girl at the party. But I'm a priest, and I'm afraid of what people think. I'm still quite young, you know. Do you understand?'

She shook her head.

'People might say that I was interested in you as a man, not as a priest.'

'Father!'

'And although you're not a little girl now, Meggie, you haven't learnt to hide the way you feel.'

She stared at him. 'Yes, I see. I didn't realize.'

'Why don't you go home now? Your family mustn't know you've been out all night.'

She got up. 'Yes, I'll go. But I wish people didn't think like that. You're not that kind of man, are you?'

Father Ralph felt hurt. 'No, Meggie. You're right. I'm not that kind of man. Go home!'

Her face was sad. 'Good night, Father.'

He kissed her hand. 'Good night, dearest Meggie.'

He watched her walk away across the grass, then he turned and went back to the big house.

♦

In the late afternoon the **housekeeper**, Mrs Smith, woke him up.

'What is it, Mrs Smith?'

'It's Mrs Carson, Father. She's dead.'

Father Ralph got up quickly and hurried to Mary Carson's room. The windows of the room were closed and she had been dead for many hours. The smell was terrible and there were flies everywhere.

'Quick, Mrs Smith! Open the windows!' he said as he moved towards the bed, his face white. 'Then go to Mr Cleary. We must bury her as soon as we can.'

Father Ralph returned to his room and remembered the letter Mary Carson had given him. Downstairs he could hear the servants running about, getting the house ready. He took out the envelope and opened it. There was a letter and a **will** inside.

25

My dearest Ralph,

You will see that there is a will with this letter. There is another will in Harry Gough's office in Gillanbone. This is a later one.

Nobody knows about this will except you and me. This is the only copy. I planned it that way — after you have read the will, you will understand my plan.

When I first knew you, you came to Drogheda because you wanted my money. Then later, you came because you wanted to be with Meggie. But did you ever realize how much money I had? I'll tell you — I have thirteen million pounds.

Read my will, Ralph, and then decide what you are going to do about it. You can give it to Harry Gough or you can burn it. The old will in Harry's office leaves everything I have to Paddy.

I know that making this decision will hurt you, Ralph.

She hadn't signed the letter. Although the priest wanted to burn the letter and the will, without reading the will at all, he knew he couldn't do it. He had to know what was in the will.

The will left all her money to the Church, because of Mary Carson's respect for Father Ralph. Father Ralph de Bricassart would be responsible for looking after the money and Drogheda. Drogheda must never be sold, and Padraic Cleary would continue to manage it and live in the big house. Father Ralph de Bricassart would receive ten thousand pounds a year for the rest of his life.

Father Ralph stopped reading and looked out of the window. Thirteen million pounds! With all that money the Church wouldn't be able to ignore him.

Paddy and his family had worked hard for Mary Carson for seven years and never complained. Paddy loved Drogheda; it should be his.

But with thirteen million pounds Father Ralph would at last have a chance to be Cardinal de Bricassart. What about Paddy,

Fee, the boys and Meggie? How well Mary Carson had understood them all! Paddy would be angry, but he wouldn't try to change the will.

Father Ralph stood up and went to the door of his room. He knew already what his decision would be.

Paddy was waiting for him downstairs.

'Oh, Father!' he said. 'Isn't it awful! What am I going to do?'

'Have you seen the body? She'll have to be buried early tomorrow morning. I'll have to go back to Gillanbone tonight.'

'Come back as soon as you can, Father!' Paddy said.

In Gillanbone, Father Ralph drove to Harry Gough's house. The lawyer was sitting down to dinner.

'Mary Carson is dead, Harry.'

'She'll be buried tomorrow? I'll phone people and tell them. And tell Paddy I'll come tomorrow and bring Mary's will with me.'

'I'm afraid there's a problem,' said the priest. 'Mary made another will, you see. She gave me the envelope last night. When I opened it today I found a new will.'

'Mary made a new will? Without me?'

'Yes. Here it is.' The priest took out the will and handed it to the lawyer.

When he had read the new will, Harry looked up at the priest. His eyes showed Father Ralph how he felt.

'Well, Father, congratulations! You've got everything. Is this the only copy of the will?'

'I think so.'

'Then why didn't you destroy it and make sure that Paddy got it all? Why should the Church have everything?'

The priest spoke calmly. 'But that wouldn't be right. Mary could do whatever she liked with her own money.'

◆

It was four in the morning when Father Ralph returned from Gillanbone. Meggie was waiting for him.

'Are you all right, Father?'

'Yes, but I don't want to go inside the house yet. Will you ride with me?'

As they rode beside the river, Father Ralph realized that soon his superiors in the Church would need him to go to Sydney. Well, it would be better that way. They stopped and sat down together on the river bank.

'What's the matter, Father?'

'I've sold you, my Meggie, for thirteen million pieces of silver. Sit closer, we may not have the chance to talk again. I'm going away.'

'When?' asked Meggie in a small voice.

'In a few days.'

'It'll be hard for me, Father. Harder than Frank.'

'It'll be hard for me, too. I have no-one but you. But I think perhaps it's a good thing for you that I'm going away. You mustn't dream of me – I can never feel that way about you. When I say I love you, I mean as a priest, not as a man.'

'I understand,' she said. 'But I'll miss you.' Then she put her arms around his neck and kissed him.

He pulled her arms away. 'It's time to go,' he said.

♦

Father Ralph was surprised to learn that Paddy was quite happy about Mary Carson's will. All he and the boys wanted was to stay at Drogheda.

'Let the Church have Mary's money,' said Paddy. He turned to Father Ralph. 'Father, please don't think I hate you because of this. You were very good to Mary, and you've been good to me and my family. We'll never forget it.'

And although it made Father Ralph feel guilty, he took Paddy's hand and shook it.

Then he left Drogheda and didn't come back. A new priest came to Gillanbone, and Father Ralph became secretary to the **Archbishop** in Sydney.

THREE:
1929–1932 PADDY

Chapter Eight

The Cleary family were moving into the big house. One morning, Fee started to wrap her cups in old newspapers. Suddenly she stopped, and Meggie came into the kitchen to find her mother staring at a newspaper, her face white.

'Daddy, Daddy!' she called, frightened.

Paddy picked up the paper and read aloud, his voice becoming sadder and sadder.

BOXER IN PRISON FOR LIFE

Francis Armstrong Cleary, aged 26, a boxer, was sent to prison for life. Cleary had killed another man in a street fight outside a bar.

When he was asked if he had anything to say, Cleary answered, 'Just don't tell my mother'.

Paddy looked at the date on the newspaper. 'This happened over three years ago,' he said.

For a long time no one spoke, then Fee started to cry. 'My poor, poor Frank!' she said.

Paddy wiped away her tears. 'We'll go and see him,' he said.

'I can't go,' Fee said. 'It would kill him to see me. He always wanted to be someone important. And now . . . You read the newspaper: "Just don't tell my mother". We've got to let him keep his secret.'

Paddy looked at Fee's unhappy face. 'All right, Fee. We won't go. But I'll ask Father de Bricassart to find out what's happening to Frank.'

Some colour came back into Fee's face. 'Yes, Paddy, do that,' she said softly.

After that, Paddy and the boys were especially kind to Fee, making sure that nothing else worried her. But Fee seemed to change, she wasn't interested in any of her family.

Father de Bricassart paid Paddy well for managing Drogheda, and the Cleary family had never had so much money. Father Ralph himself never came to Drogheda, but he visited Frank in prison. He found Frank very disturbed and unhappy, but when he wrote to the family he said that Frank was well and feeling calm.

Paddy wanted to sell Father Ralph's horse, which was still kept at Drogheda.

'Oh, please, Daddy,' said Meggie. 'Don't do that! What would Father Ralph think if he came back?'

'I don't think he'll come back, Meggie,' said Paddy. 'But we'll keep the horse, if you like.'

♦

It had been a dry winter, and the summer rains didn't come. The grass was dry, even the trees were dry. Meggie rode her horse across the fields and dreamed about Ralph, imagining that he was her husband. She couldn't understand why he didn't come and see her.

'Daddy,' she asked one day. 'Why doesn't Father de Bricassart ever visit us? Has he forgotten us?'

'No, not really. He often writes, doesn't he?' He turned and looked at his daughter thoughtfully. 'But I think it's best that he doesn't come, so I haven't invited him. It's wrong for you to dream about a priest, you must understand that. He still thinks of you as a little girl.'

She looked stubborn. 'But he could stop being a priest. If I could talk to him about it . . .'

Paddy's face was shocked. 'Meggie! Father de Bricassart is a priest. He can never, never stop being a priest, understand that. He's promised the Church, and he can never break that promise.'

Without a word, Meggie turned her horse and rode away.

♦

At the same time, in Sydney, Father Ralph was working hard, and impressing his superiors in the Church. Nevertheless, he sometimes found it hard to stop himself taking the train to Drogheda to see the people there, especially Meggie.

Chapter Nine

In the winter of 1932 the dry storms came back. Paddy was far away from the house when the biggest storm came that day in August. He got off his horse and sat under a tree to wait until the storm was over.

It was a terrible storm. Suddenly Paddy saw an enormous tree burst into blue flames. He jumped to his feet and saw everything around him catch fire. He didn't have time to reach his horse. In every direction there were walls of fire. He heard his horse scream, and suddenly he knew it was the end. There was no way out of the fire for him or for his horse and dogs.

♦

All the other men had returned to Drogheda before the storm began, and they waited indoors for it to end. At about four o'clock the clouds rolled away, and everybody felt better. Jack and Bob went outside to look around.

'Look!' said Bob, pointing to the west.

Above the trees they could see a great cloud of smoke rising into the sky.

'Good God!' Jack cried, running inside to the telephone.

'Fire, fire!' he shouted into the phone. 'Fire on Drogheda, and a big one!'

Everyone knew what to do. The boys ran for their horses, and the other workers ran out of their houses. As Meggie rode beside Fee, the cloud of smoke in the west grew, and they could smell burning on the wind. Animals running from the fire passed them as they rode towards the fire. The fire had already travelled ten miles and it was five miles wide. It was too late to save most of the sheep.

Their neighbours arrived in cars, eager to help.

'How big is it, Bob?' one asked,

'Too big to fight,' said Bob. 'It's travelling too fast. I don't know if we can save the houses.'

'Where's your father, Bob?'

'West of the fire. He was working with some sheep out there.'

The wind was still strong, and there was a smell of burning everywhere. Night fell, but to the west the sky was bright with flames. From the house Meggie heard the roar of the fire, and saw trees burst into flame. She could see the figures of men running in front of the burning trees. Then the wind changed and the fire rushed away to the east. The big house was saved.

◆

For three days the fire continued, travelling east and spreading wider as it went. Then there was a heavy fall of rain that lasted for four days, and put out the fire. But it had gone a hundred miles, ~nd it had left a blackened path twenty miles wide.

No-one expected to hear from Paddy until the rain started. The fire had brought down the telephone line, and the ground was too hot to cross. But after the rain had fallen for six hours they began to worry.

He ought to be here by now,' said Bob. 'I think we should go and look for him.'

Fee was anxious. 'I'll come with you. Meggie can come too. We're going to need all the people we can get.'

They rode across the river and into the area of the fire. Everything was black; even after all the rain, steam rose from the hot ground. Bob and Meggie rode in front, then Jack and Hughie, and finally Fee and Stuart. They stayed close together and didn't talk. They expected to see Paddy riding towards them, but they saw nothing moving in the black land.

Then they realized that the fire had begun farther away than they first thought. Bob turned his horse and spoke to them.

'We'll start looking here. I'll go west. If you find anything, shoot three times in the air. Jack, you go south, Hughie, go south-west. Mum and Meggie, go north-west. Stu, you go north. And go slowly, everyone. Good luck!'

They rode off through the grey rain. After Stuart had gone half a mile he saw the black shapes of Paddy's horse and Paddy's dogs. He got off his horse and made his way towards them through the mud. He said a prayer as he moved through the sticky blackness. And then, not far from the horse, he found the blackened shape of a man, the arms stretched wide. Stuart raised his gun and shot three times into the air.

He didn't see the great wild pig at first as it came out of the trees. The shooting had disturbed it, and it was in pain, wounded by the fire. Stu reached for his gun, but then realized it was empty. The pig looked at him for a moment, then rushed

The pig looked at him for a moment, then rushed towards him.

towards him. Stuart hurried to load his gun, and fired. The animal was hit, but it was too late, it fell on top of him in the black mud.

◆

'I wonder why Stu hasn't fired again?' Meggie asked her mother. Fee felt anxious, and made her horse go faster. But Jack and Bob had got there first.

'Don't go in there, Mum,' said Bob.

Jack went to Meggie, and held her arms.

'Paddy?' asked Fee.

'Yes. And Stu.'

Neither of her sons could look at her.

'Daddy got caught in the fire. He's dead. Stu must have disturbed a wild pig, and it attacked him. He shot it, but it fell on him. He's dead, too, Mum.'

Meggie screamed and struggled, but Fee stood still, like a stone.

'It's too much,' she said at last.

Jack took Meggie back to the house, and returned with a cart to bring the two bodies back.

Meggie stayed at the house, and the housekeeper, Mrs Smith, tears running down her face, watched as the girl sat silently, unable to eat or speak. There was a knock on the door, and Mrs Smith went to answer it.

Father Ralph stood outside in the rain, wet and muddy.

'May I come in, Mrs Smith?'

'Oh, Father, Father!' she cried. 'How did you know?'

'Mrs Cleary sent me a message about the fire. I've got permission to come here and see if everything is all right. It's good to be back. But Mrs Smith, why are you crying?'

'Then you don't know!' she cried.

'What? Know what? What is it – what's happened?'

'Mr Cleary and Stuart are dead.'

His face went white, and he pushed the housekeeper away. 'Where's Meggie?' he asked.

'She's in there. Mrs Cleary and the boys are out. They're bringing in the bodies.'

But Father Ralph wasn't listening to her; he rushed into the room.

'Meggie!' he said, taking the girl's cold hands in his.

She fell into his arms. In spite of her pain, she felt happy, knowing that he had come back to her.

'You've come,' she said.

'Yes, I've come. Oh, Meggie, your father and Stu! How did it happen?'

Meggie told him, and he said no more. He held her in his arms, and comforted her. Then without thinking, he bent down and kissed her lips. Then he kissed her again and again. At last, he pushed her away.

'Meggie, I love you, I always will. But I'm a priest, I can't . . . I just can't!'

She stood up quickly and smiled at him.

'I'll go and find something for you to eat.'

♦

At last, Paddy and Stu were buried and Father Ralph got ready to leave. Fee was sitting at her desk, looking at her hands.

'Fee, will you be all right?' he asked.

'Yes, Father. I have work to do, and five sons left – six, if you count Frank. Thank you for looking after him.'

'Fee, what about your daughter? Do you ever remember that you have a daughter?'

'No, it's her sons a mother remembers. Do you know something, Father? Two days ago I discovered that I loved Paddy, but it was like all of my life – too late. I couldn't tell him how much I loved him.'

'Will you promise me something, Fee?'

'If you like.'

'Look after Meggie, don't forget her. Make her go to dances and meet a few young men. Encourage her to think of marriage and a home of her own.'

'Whatever you say, Father.' Fee did not move, but continued looking at her hands.

Father Ralph sighed and left the room.

Meggie was waiting for him as he went for his horse.

'Look what I found, Father,' she said and gave him a rose, the only one not destroyed by the fire. 'It's something to help you to remember me.'

He took the flower and looked down at it. 'I don't need any help to remember you, Meggie. But Meggie, I want you to forget me. I want you to look around and find a good kind man, marry him, have babies. You'll be a good mother. I can never leave the Church and I don't want to leave the Church. I don't love you the way a husband will. Forget me, Meggie!'

'Won't you kiss me goodbye?'

But Father Ralph just jumped on his horse and rode away.

FOUR:
1933–1938 LUKE

Chapter Ten

The grass grew again at Drogheda, and the work on the farm continued. Ralph de Bricassart was now Bishop Ralph. Fee never showed his letters to Meggie and forgot about her promise to him to make sure that Meggie went to dances. Meggie was invited to dances and parties, but she always refused to go. Young men would visit Drogheda, hoping to get to know Meggie, but Meggie wasn't interested in them.

◆

One day Bob told them that a new worker was coming. 'He sounds like a good man. He knows all about sheep and horses.'

'Is the new man married?' asked Fee.

'Don't know, didn't ask,' said Bob. 'He'll be here tomorrow.'

Several weeks passed before Meggie saw the new man. His name was Luke O'Neill, and her brothers often talked about him. Mrs Smith liked him, too. When Meggie finally met him he was riding towards her on a big horse.

'G-day!' he called, taking off his hat, and looking at her with laughing blue eyes. 'You must be the daughter. I'm Luke O'Neill.'

Meggie said something quickly and then became silent. She couldn't think of anything to say; Luke O'Neill's face and eyes were just like Father Ralph's.

Luke O'Neill looked at Meggie carefully, as he rode beside her. She was beautiful, all right! That hair! But why did she look so disappointed when she looked into his eyes? Luke was used to being popular with women; they didn't often look at him like that.

She looked at him again, disappointed and puzzled.

Luke smiled. 'What's the matter?'

'I'm sorry, I didn't mean to stare. You reminded me of someone, that's all.'

'Who?'

'It's not important.'

'What's your name, little Miss Cleary?'

'Meggie.'

'Meggie? That's a child's name. What is it really? Margaret?'

'No, Meghann.'

'That's better. I'll call you Meghann.'

'No, you won't. I hate it!'

But he only laughed. 'I'll call you anything I like.'

A week later Meggie met Luke again.

'Good afternoon, Meghann.'

'Good afternoon.'

'There's a dance next Saturday night. Will you come with me?'

'Thank you for asking me, but I can't dance.'

'Don't worry. I'll teach you. And Bob would let me borrow a car.'

'I said I wouldn't go!' she said.

'No, you said you couldn't dance, and I said I'd teach you.'

Meggie looked at him angrily.

'You always get everything you want, don't you, Meghann?'

◆

Bob was surprised when Luke asked him for the car, but he handed over the keys.

'I never thought of Meggie going to a dance, but take her! Perhaps she'll like it. She doesn't go out much.'

'Why don't you and Jack and Hughie come, too?' Luke asked.

Bob shook his head. 'No, thanks. We don't like dances much.'

'I think you're the most beautiful girl I've ever seen,' said Luke to Meggie as he started the car that evening.

Meggie said nothing.

'Isn't this nice?' Luke asked. 'This is the life, no doubt about it.'

'You won't leave me alone, will you?' she asked.

'Of course not! You've come with me, haven't you? That means you're mine all night long.'

Everyone in the district was at the dance. The other women looked at Luke with envy, but he never left Meggie alone the whole evening. She enjoyed dancing with him, and liked the way he held her in his strong arms.

They didn't speak much as they drove home. It was seventy miles to Drogheda. The car climbed a little hill, then Luke stopped it and they got out. It was so quiet, so far from anyone! They stood together, under the stars.

'Were you born here, Meghann?' Luke asked.

'No, I was born in New Zealand. We came here thirteen years ago.'

'I'd like to take you to all the dances.'

'Thank you.'

They stood and looked out over the dark countryside. Then Meggie sighed and they returned to the car. Luke did not try to kiss Meggie. He was too wise; he planned to marry her if he could, and he didn't want to frighten her. He would wait until she wanted to be kissed.

There were other dances, and the people at Drogheda understood that Meggie now had a very good-looking boyfriend. Meggie thought about Luke a lot, and she stopped comparing him with Father Ralph. She knew that Father Ralph was Bishop Ralph now, and he would never come back to her. She didn't like any of the other young men she knew as much as she liked Luke.

Although they talked a lot, Luke never seemed to be interested in Meggie's life. Luke was clever, he worked hard and he was hungry to be rich. His family were poor, and his father had died when Luke was twelve years old. Luke had found a job immediately, and he had worked hard ever since. He wanted to be successful and he wanted to be rich. He was disappointed to learn that Meggie's family didn't own Drogheda, but he had also learnt that Meggie had some money of her own. And it was money, more than land, that Luke wanted.

◆

The thirteenth dance Luke took Meggie to was in Gillanbone. It was a cold night, winter was coming. Luke put his arm around Meggie as they stood beside the car.

'You're cold,' he said. 'I'd better get you home.'

'No, it's all right now. I'm getting warm.'

Meggie wanted love. She wanted to know what Luke's kisses were like. Luke turned and kissed her, but Meggie was disappointed. She didn't feel the way she had expected to feel.

They got back into the car. Luke was aware that his kiss hadn't succeeded. He didn't want to frighten Meggie. Well, he would try something else.

For a while they sat in silence.

'I'm sorry, Luke,' she said.

'I'm sorry, too, Meghann. Don't worry about it. I didn't mean to frighten you.'

When they got back he kissed her very gently. She seemed to like that, he thought. He was glad that he hadn't ruined his chances.

The second time Luke kissed her, Meggie behaved quite differently. They had been to a wonderful party, and they had enjoyed their evening together. It was a long way home and very cold. The car was warm, and they had some wine to drink and some sandwiches to eat.

'You look very pretty tonight, Meghann.'

Luke took off his tie.

'Oh, that feels good! Much more comfortable.'

Then he turned and kissed her, gently at first, and then harder. Her arms went around him, and held him tightly. It felt so warm, so good.

He sighed. 'You'd better marry me, Meghann' he said, eyes soft and laughing. 'We can't be alone together, it's too dangerous. What would your brothers think?'

'Yes, I think I'd better, too,' she agreed, her cheeks pink.

'Let's tell them tomorrow morning.'

'Why not?'

'Then next Saturday I'll drive into Gillanbone and see the priest. You'll want to be married in church. And I'll buy a ring.'

'Thank you, Luke.'

No-one was very surprised at the news. They were surprised when Meggie refused to write and tell Bishop Ralph, or invite him to the wedding. She didn't want to have a big wedding, either.

So Fee promised Meggie that she wouldn't mention the wedding in her letters to Bishop Ralph. She didn't seem to be interested herself in the wedding or in the man Meggie had chosen to marry.

Chapter Eleven

The wedding was to be on Saturday August 25th, in the church in Gillanbone.

'Darling, I've decided where to take you after our wedding,' said Luke.

'Where?'

'North Queensland. I was talking to some men in the hotel, and they were telling me that you can make a lot of money up there cutting **sugar cane**.'

'But Luke, you've got a good job here!'

'I don't feel right living with your family. I want to get us the money to buy a place of our own in Western Queensland.'

'Does this mean you're thinking of making our home in Queensland, Luke?'

'Yes.'

Meggie stared out of the window. Not to live at Drogheda! To be somewhere where Bishop Ralph would never visit, to live without seeing him again . . . Her eyes looked at Luke's eager face and grew sadder. But her sadness didn't worry him, he didn't worry about what she wanted. No woman, even one as beautiful as Meggie Cleary, was going to tell him what to do.

'Meghann,' he said. 'I believe that when a man and a woman marry, all the woman's property should become the man's. I know you've got a bit of money, and when we marry I'll expect you to give it to me.'

'Of course,' said Meggie. The idea didn't seem strange to her.

'How much money have you got?' he asked.

'At the moment, fourteen thousand pounds. Every year I get two thousand more.'

He whistled. 'Fourteen thousand! That's a lot of money, Meghann. I'd better look after it for you. We can see the bank manager next week. I'm not going to touch any of it, you know that. I'll save it to buy our farm later on. For the next few years we're both going to work hard, and save all the money we earn. All right?'

She nodded. 'Yes, Luke.'

◆

Meggie and Luke were married very quietly in Gillanbone and they left the same evening on the long train journey to North Queensland.

They spent the first night of their marriage sitting on the crowded slow train which went north-east to Goondiwindi. When they got there they had to wait for another train. There was nothing to eat or drink at the station because it was Sunday. They changed trains again at Brisbane. Once again they had to sit up because Luke had bought second class seats.

'But Luke, we've got enough money,' said Meggie. 'Why couldn't we travel first class and sleep on the train?'

Luke stared at her, surprised. 'But it's only three days and three nights! Why spend money when we're both young and healthy? Remember, I'm not a rich man!'

Meggie sat beside the window and looked out. Luke seemed to think that she was a child, but she was too proud to argue. She wanted to be a good wife, and she remembered how her father had loved her mother. In time, Luke would be the same.

The train was crowded as it made its way slowly northwards. Meggie's head ached, and she felt sick. It grew hotter and hotter, and her lovely new dress became dirty. She almost hated Luke, who didn't seem to be tired at all.

Late on Thursday afternoon they got off the train. Meggie could hardly walk. Luke asked at the station for the address of a cheap hotel, picked up their cases and went off down the street.

Their room was small and full of ugly old furniture, but it seemed like heaven to Meggie. She fell onto the bed.

'Lie down for a while, love,' said Luke. 'I'm going out to look around.'

Meggie lay her head on the pillow, and fell asleep.

♦

She slept for two days. When she woke up, Luke was sitting at the window, smoking.

'How do you feel now?' he asked.

Meggie sat up slowly and stretched her arms. 'I feel much better now, thank you. Oh Luke! I know I'm young and strong, but I'm not as strong as you are.'

He came to sit beside her on the bed. 'I'm sorry, Meghann. I'm not used to having a wife with me, that's all. Are you hungry?'

'Very hungry. It's almost a week since I've eaten.'

'Well, have a bath, put on a clean dress, and let's go out.'

They had a Chinese meal at a restaurant near the hotel,

then walked around the town. The buildings were white, and there were trees and plants growing everywhere. It was completely different from Gillanbone, and very, very hot. Meggie noticed that all the other women were wearing tiny shorts and tops. The air felt so hot and wet Meggie could hardly breathe.

'Luke, can we go back now?' she asked after a while.

'If you want to.'

♦

'I've got you a job,' Luke said over breakfast in the hotel dining room the next day.

'What? We haven't even got a house yet, Luke!'

'We don't need a house, Meg. I'm going to cut sugar cane; it's all arranged. I'll be living with the cane cutters, and we work six days a week. I could earn twenty pounds a week!'

'Do you mean we're not going to live together?'

'We can't, Meg! The men won't have a woman living with them. You don't need to live alone in a house. If you work too, we'll have more money for our own house. I've found you a job as a housekeeper. You can live there, and all your money will go into the bank.'

'But when will I see you, Luke?'

'On Sundays. They'll let you go out on Sundays.'

'Well, you've arranged everything, haven't you?'

'Yes. Oh, Meg, we're going to be rich! You'd like that, wouldn't you?'

'If it's what you want.' Meggie looked in her bag for the money that Bob had given her before she left Drogheda. 'Luke, where's my hundred pounds?'

'I put it in the bank. You won't need any money when you're working. It's out in the country; there's nothing to spend money on. I'm not going to spend any money, either. It's all for our future.'

In the morning they went out to Himmelhoch, the farm where Meggie was going to work.

'That's very sensible, Luke. But what if I have a baby?'

Luke had planned not to have any children until they bought their farm, but he decided not to tell Meggie.

'Well, let's wait and see what happens,' he said.

In the morning they went out to Himmelhoch, the farm where Meggie was going to work. It was a large white house on top of a hill. Anne Mueller, the farmer's wife, was waiting for them. She had a kind face, and smiled at Meggie.

'Call me Anne,' she said. 'I hope you're going to like living with us, Meggie. I hope you won't find the weather too hot for you. And I hope you won't miss your big handsome husband too much.'

Meggie didn't answer. Miss Luke? She didn't think so. But he *was* her husband. Perhaps things would be better when they got their own farm. He wasn't a bad man, but he had been alone for so long he didn't know how to share his life with another person. He didn't try to understand what she needed. Still, things could be worse; Anne Mueller was warm and friendly.

As for Luke, he soon settled down to the work of cutting sugar cane. He loved the work, and he enjoyed being with the other men.

◆

Meggie didn't see Luke again for four weeks. Each Sunday she put on a pretty dress and waited for him, but he didn't come. Anne and Luddie Mueller didn't say anything, but they watched her disappointment growing.

On the fourth Sunday, he came. Anne Mueller greeted him as he came into the house.

'I'm glad you've remembered that you have a wife,' she said. 'Come in and have breakfast with us. I was beginning to think you weren't going to come and see Meggie.'

'Well, I decided to work on Sundays, too. Tomorrow we're leaving the district.'

47

'So Meggie won't see you so often.'

'Meg understands,' said Luke. 'There'll be a holiday in the summer. I might take Meg to Sydney then.'

Luddie, Anne and Luke continued to talk about Luke's plans, but Meggie didn't speak. She drank her tea and listened. First Luke said they would get a farm in two years, now he was saying that it would be four or five years. Luke loved his life at present; would he ever give it up? How long would she have to wait? The Muellers were very kind to her, and she didn't have to work hard. But the weather at Himmelhoch made her feel tired and ill. Why couldn't she wait for Luke at Drogheda?

After breakfast Luke took her for a walk through the fields.

'Do you think we could have a little house after a year or two, Luke?' she asked.

'Why? You don't want to be on your own, do you? Aren't you happy here?'

'Yes, but I want my own home.'

'Look, Meg, you know we've got to save our money. Do you hear me?'

'Yes, Luke.'

And so Luke left her at Himmelhoch. He intended to kiss her before he left, but in the end, he forgot.

'Poor little thing!' said Anne to Luddie. 'I could kill him!'

◆

When the summer came, Luke went to Sydney, but he didn't take Meggie with him. Back at Himmelhoch, the weather got hotter and the rain fell every day. Meggie wished more and more that she was at home at Drogheda. She felt that she would never grow to love North Queensland, but she couldn't see how she would ever escape. She dreamed of Drogheda, but she was too proud to tell her family how her husband neglected her.

The months passed, then a year went by. Meggie had been at

Himmelhoch for two whole years. Luke had visited her only six times. One Sunday Luke arrived to take Meggie to a dance. When they arrived at the dance Meggie was left in a corner with some other women. Luke spent most of the evening drinking and talking to his friends.

'Well, did you enjoy that?' asked Luke as he drove Meggie home.

'I didn't dance very often,' she answered.

'Well, excuse me!' said Luke, coldly. 'I thought you might like it. I didn't have to take you!'

'I don't think you really want me to be part of your life,' said Meggie. 'I'm tired of living like this. I never see you alone. I want to go home to Drogheda!'

But Luke remembered Meggie's two thousand pounds a year.

'Oh, Meg!' he said. 'It won't be for ever, I promise! And this summer I will take you to Sydney. We can live there for three months and have a wonderful time!'

Meggie looked at him, as the moon shone on his handsome face, so much like Ralph de Bricassart's. She still wanted his babies. 'All right,' she said. 'All right. I'll wait another year. And I must go to Sydney with you this time!'

Chapter Twelve

Meggie wrote to Fee, Bob and the boys once a month. She never mentioned that anything was wrong between her and Luke. Her family thought that the Muellers were friends and that Meggie was staying with them because Luke was away so often. They didn't know that Meggie was working as their house-keeper. They were sorry that she didn't come to visit them at Drogheda; they didn't realize that she had no money for the train.

Sometimes in her letters Meggie asked a question about

Bishop Ralph, and occasionally Bob would remember to tell her something about him. Then came a letter full of news of the Bishop.

'He suddenly arrived here,' Bob wrote, 'looking rather upset. He was surprised not to find you here and he was angry because nobody told him about you and Luke. I think he missed you. He asked if you had any children. I hope you have some soon, because I think Bishop Ralph would like that. I offered to give him your address, but he said no. He said he was going to Greece. He didn't stay long at Drogheda.'

Meggie put the letter down. Ralph knew, he knew! What had he thought about it? Why had this happened to her? She didn't love Luke, she never would love Luke. What a mess their lives were!

◆

In Athens, Ralph de Bricassart was thinking about Meggie. Perhaps now he would never see her again. Was she happy? Was Luke O'Neill good to her? Did she love him? What kind of man was he? Had Meggie married Luke to make Ralph feel bad? Why didn't they have any children?

Soon Bishop Ralph's work in Greece was over and he was sent to Rome. After six months he returned to Australia. He was now an Archbishop, and more than ever, the Church had become his life.

◆

At the end of August, Meggie got a letter from Luke. He was in hospital, but he wasn't seriously ill. However he couldn't return to work until he was better. He suggested that he and Meggie should go away together for a holiday.

Meggie could hardly believe it. She didn't really know if she wanted to be alone with Luke any more. But this might be her chance to have a baby. If she had a child to love, life would be so much easier Anne would love to have a baby in the house, too. So would Luddie.

Luke borrowed a car and drove Meggie into the mountains. The weather was cool, and they stayed in a small hotel beside a beautiful lake.

'We only need five thousand pounds more, then we can buy our farm,' Luke told her.

'I could write to Bishop de Bricassart. He'll lend us the money.'

'No, you won't!' he said angrily. 'We'll work for what we have, Meg, not borrow!'

Meggie had never felt so angry. Luke had taken everything away from her, and she didn't believe he ever wanted to be a farmer. He was quite happy with his life. He didn't want her to have a home or a baby.

Luke soon recovered from his illness. He ate well, and he began to look healthier. Meggie persuaded him to stay there a week longer, then for another week. After a month he decided it was time to return to work.

'We can't sit here spending money, Meg,' he said.

Luke was eager to get back to the sugar cane and his friends. The only thing Meggie could hope for was that after a whole month together she was expecting a baby. Then Luke might change his mind and make a home for them.

So she went back to Himmelhoch and waited, praying for a baby. When her prayers were answered Anne and Luddie were delighted.

Meggie felt very ill. As the months passed, the doctor began to worry about her. He decided she must go to the hospital before the baby was born.

'And try to get her husband to come to see her!' the doctor said to Luddie.

When Meggie wrote to Luke to tell him about the baby, she

51

expected he would be happy. But Luke sent an angry reply; the baby would cost him money, and Meggie wouldn't be able to work.

Meggie wanted to go home to Drogheda, but she was too weak to travel. She knew now that having the baby wouldn't change Luke. He had married her for her money, and she had married him because she wanted to escape from Ralph de Bricassart. There had been no real love between them.

She was thinking of Luke and Ralph one day, and wondering why she had married Luke, when it was Ralph she really loved. How could she be happy with Luke O'Neill's child? How different she would feel if the baby was Ralph's!

Suddenly she stood up and went to look for Anne.

'Anne, phone Doctor Smith. The baby's coming now!'

The doctor hurried out to Himmelhoch in his small car. He brought a nurse with him.

'Have you let the husband know?' he asked.

'I've sent him a message,' said Anne. 'This way, Doctor. She's in my room.'

Hours later, the doctor came out of the room.

'It's a long, hard business. She should be in hospital. She's very brave. She keeps asking if Ralph's here yet. I thought her husband's name was Luke?'

'It is.'

Anne looked out of the window. In the distance, she saw a taxi approaching. There was a black-haired man in the back.

'I don't believe it. Luke's coming at last.'

The doctor returned to the bedroom. 'I won't say anything to Mrs O'Neill,' he said. 'It might not be her husband.'

The taxi stopped, and Anne was surprised to see a tall man, wearing the clothes of an archbishop, get out. Was Luke playing some strange joke? But when the man turned, she realized he was ten years older than Luke.

'Mrs Mueller?' he asked. 'I'm Archbishop Ralph de Bricassart. I believe Mrs Luke O'Neill is staying with you.'

So this was Ralph, Anne thought. 'Yes, sir,' she said.

'I'm a very old friend of hers. May I see her, please?'

'I'm sure she'd be delighted to see you, Archbishop, but at the moment she's having a baby. She's having a very hard time.'

Anne could see there was deep feeling in the Archbishop's blue eyes. What was there between this man and Meggie? she wondered.

'I *knew* something was wrong!' he cried. 'Please let me see her! If you need a reason, I am a priest.'

Anne didn't want to stop him seeing Meggie. 'Come along, through here,' she said.

He went past Doctor Smith and the nurse without seeing them and knelt beside the bed to take Meggie's hand.

'Meggie!'

Meggie opened her eyes, full of pain, and saw him.

'Ralph, help me,' she said. 'Pray for me, and the baby. You can save us. You are closer to God than we are. No one wants us, not even you.'

'Where's Luke?'

'I don't know, and I don't care.' She closed her eyes in pain, but she didn't let go of his hand.

The doctor touched his shoulder. 'I think you ought to go outside now, sir.'

'If there's any danger, you'll call me.'

'Of course.'

Ralph left the bedroom and joined Anne and Luddie.

'How long have you known Meggie?' Luddie asked him.

'Since she first arrived in Australia from New Zealand. But I feel as if I've known her for ever.'

'You love her!' said Anne, surprised.

'Always.'

'How sad for you both.'

'I always hoped it was only sad for me. Tell me about Meggie. What's happened to her since she married? I haven't seen her for many years, but I haven't been happy about her.'

'Luddie and I know nothing about her life before she came to Queensland,' said Anne. 'I think she's too proud to talk about it.'

So the Archbishop told them about Meggie's life at Drogheda.

Anne was shocked. 'Imagine! Luke O'Neill took her away from that life and made her work here as a servant. *And* he made us put all the money she earned in his bank! Do you realize she hasn't had any money to spend since she came to live here?'

'Don't feel sorry for Meggie,' said Archbishop Ralph, his voice hard. 'I don't think she feels sorry for herself. And I'm sure she doesn't mind about the money. Money hasn't brought her happiness, has it? I think she cares more that Luke doesn't seem to love her. My poor Meggie!'

When Anne and Luddie had finished telling him about Meggie's life in Queensland, the Archbishop sighed. 'Well, we must help her, if Luke won't. Maybe she'd better go back to Drogheda. I shall send you a cheque from Sydney for her – she won't want to ask her brother for money. Dear God, let the child be born soon.'

But the child wasn't born until twenty-four hours later. Meggie was almost dead with exhaustion and pain. Doctor Smith came out of the bedroom.

'Well, it's all over,' he said. 'Meggie is very ill, but she'll be all right. And the baby is small, but very strong. Her hair is bright red, and she's got a terrible temper.'

Archbishop Ralph went with Luddie and Anne to see the new mother. Meggie looked very small and weak in the big bed. The baby was crying loudly.

Ralph took Meggie's hand. 'She's a strong baby,' he said, smiling.

'I don't think she likes life much,' said Meggie. Then she turned to Anne and Luddie. 'My dear good friends! What would I have done without you? Have we heard from Luke?'

'He sent a message. He was too busy to come, but he wished you good luck.' Anne bent and kissed Meggie. 'We'll leave you alone with the Archbishop, dear.'

'What are you going to call your noisy daughter?' he asked as the door closed.

'Justine.'

'Don't you want her, Meggie?'

'I did want her, but now I feel she doesn't want me.'

'I must go, Meggie,' he said gently.

Her eyes grew harder and brighter. 'I knew you'd want to go! You're just like Luke! You can't wait to get away from me!'

He looked hurt. 'Please don't feel like that, Meggie. Don't change, don't become hard. You were always so sweet and gentle. You wouldn't be my Meggie any more.'

But still she looked at him as if she hated him. 'No, Ralph! I'm not your Meggie, I never was. You didn't want me, so I married Luke. You've spoiled my life! I've loved you for years, and wanted no one but you, and waited for you . . . I tried so hard to forget you, then I married a man who looked like you, and he doesn't want me either!'

She began to cry, then stopped.

'Luke's not a bad man,' she continued. 'He's just a man, like you. He wants something, and he doesn't care about hurting other people to get what he wants.'

He didn't know what to say to her, because he had never seen her like this before.

'Do you remember the rose you gave me at Drogheda?' he asked gently.

'Yes, I remember,' she answered, her voice lifeless.

'I still have it. Every time I see a rose that colour I think of you. Meggie, I love you. You're my rose, the most beautiful thing in my life.'

Her eyes again became hard and bright. 'You can only dream, can't you, Ralph de Bricassart? You don't know anything about real human life. You say you love me, but you've got no idea what love really is; you're just saying the words!'

'Meggie, don't! Please don't!'

'Oh, go away! I don't want to look at you!'

He left the room without looking back.

♦

Luke never answered the message that told him that he was the father of a baby girl. Meggie slowly began to get better, and the baby grew. But although Meggie took care of the baby, she didn't feel much love for her.

The months passed, and still Luke stayed away. Meggie wrote to him often, but he didn't answer her letters. The baby was healthier than Meggie, who looked tired and ill. One day Anne came to her with an offer.

'Meggie, Luddie and I are worried about you. You're not well, and you aren't eating properly. So we've booked you a holiday. The Archbishop sent a big cheque for you when the baby was born, and so did your brother. You need a holiday and you need time to think. So we've arranged for you to go to Matlock Island for two months. Luddie and I will look after Justine.'

'Anne, you and Luddie have cared for me so well; much more than Luke has. You're right, I'm not well,' Meggie said. 'Oh, Anne, I'm so tired! I'm not a good mother to Justine, and I ought to be. She didn't ask to be born. And Luke won't even give me a chance to try to love him. He doesn't seem to love me, and I think it's my fault.'

'It's the Archbishop you love, isn't it?'

'Oh, yes, since I was a little girl! I said some hard things to him when he was here. Poor Ralph! He never encouraged me to love him, you know. Oh, why does the Church say that it's wrong for me to love Ralph?'

'Maybe you could persuade Luke to buy a farm, Meggie.'

'No, he doesn't really want one. All he wants is to live as he lives now. He likes cutting sugar cane; he likes his friends. He doesn't want a home, but I do. I'm just an ordinary woman, I want my own home, and I want love from someone.'

'I understand,' said Anne.

'I'll go to Matlock Island,' Meggie said. 'I'm very grateful to you for thinking of it. What kind of place is it?'

'It's a small island, very quiet and private. You can stay in a little cottage of your own. You won't see many other people there at this time of year. You'll have a chance to do some thinking about your future.'

Chapter Thirteen

Meggie started her journey to Matlock island on the last day of 1937. She was twenty-six years old. She arrived there in the evening, an hour before the sun went down. An old man was waiting for her.

'How d'you do, Mrs O'Neill,' he greeted her. 'I'm Rob Walter. I hope your husband'll be able to join you here. There aren't a lot of people here this time of year; they all come in the winter.'

They drove along a narrow road through the trees.

'Oh, how beautiful!' said Meggie.

They had come out on another road which ran along beside the beach. The water was like silver, still and calm.

'The island's four miles wide and eight miles long,' Mr Walter explained. 'We live in that white house, but your cottage is further away. When you need something, pick up your phone and I'll bring it.'

The cottage had its own private beach, and here the road ended. Inside it was very plain, but comfortable. There was food in the refrigerator, and a wide, comfortable bed. Meggie would be able to eat well and sleep well.

◆

For the first week she seemed to do nothing but eat and sleep; she hadn't realized how exhausted she was. She wasn't at all lonely, she didn't miss Anne or Luddie or Justine or Luke, and she didn't even think about Drogheda. Old Rob never disturbed her.

She thought about herself, and about her plans for the future. She really wanted Ralph, but she couldn't have him. She decided that she must try to make Luke give her more children, buy her a home, let her keep her own money. She wasn't going to waste her life dreaming of a man and children she could never have. The future belonged to Luke, and to Luke's children.

Meggie lay on the beach and cried like a child; only the birds heard her.

◆

Anne Mueller had chosen Matlock Island deliberately, planning to send Luke there as soon as she could. She sent Luke a message, saying that Meggie needed him. She loved Meggie and Justine, and wanted them to be happy. Justine must have a home, and she must have both her parents.

Luke arrived at Himmelhoch two days later. He was going to Sydney, but first he wanted to see the baby. He had been disappointed that the baby was a girl; a boy would have been able to work and to help on the farm when Luke was too old to cut sugar cane.

'How's Meg?' he asked. 'Not sick, I hope.'

'No, she's not sick. I'll tell you in a minute. But first come and look at your daughter.'

Luke looked at the baby. 'She's a funny little thing,' he said. 'She doesn't look too happy, does she?'

'Why should she look happy?' said Anne. 'She's never seen her father, she hasn't got a real home and you don't seem to be planning to give her one!'

'I'm saving my money, Anne!' Luke replied.

'I know you've got enough money now, Luke. Property is cheap at the moment, and you know it.'

'It's the weather. There hasn't been enough rain for two years. I think I ought to wait.'

'Nonsense, Luke!'

'I'm not ready to leave the sugar yet,' Luke said stubbornly.

'Yes, that's the truth at last, isn't it?' said Anne, trembling with anger. 'You don't really want to be married. You don't mind if you neglect your wife and family.'

'I don't neglect them. Meg's safe, and she's got enough to eat.'

'You married Meggie for her money, didn't you?'

Luke's face turned red. He wouldn't look at Anne. 'The money helped, but I really liked Meg.'

'What about loving her?'

'What's love? Just something women imagine, that's all. Now, if you've finished, where's Meg?'

'I sent her away for a while. She wasn't well. I was hoping you'd join her, but I see that's impossible.'

'Of course it's impossible. I'm going to Sydney tonight.'

'What shall I tell Meggie when she comes back?'

Luke was eager to leave. 'I don't know. Tell her to wait a while longer. And tell her I'd like a son next time.'

Anne picked up the baby and sat down on the bed.

'Go away, Luke! You don't deserve what you've got!'

◆

The next day a postcard arrived from Meggie on Matlock Island, saying she was feeling well. Anne decided not to tell her about Luke's visit.

As Anne sat with Justine outside her house, she saw a red car coming along the road towards the farm. It stopped in front of her and a tall, handsome man, dressed only in a pair of shorts, jumped out. At first she didn't recognize him.

'Well, Archbishop,' she said. 'What a surprise!'

'At the moment I'm not an archbishop, only a priest on holiday, so you can call me Ralph. Is this Meggie's baby? May I hold her?'

Justine seemed to like the priest and fell peacefully asleep.

'Where's Meggie?' he asked.

'She's not here. Luddie and I sent her away for two months. She's got another seven weeks to go.'

Anne realized as soon as she spoke that he was disappointed.

'I came to say goodbye to her,' he said. 'I'm going to Rome. It's a great opportunity for me. I can't refuse to go.'

'How long will you be away?'

'Oh, a very long time, I think. There's going to be a war in Europe. I can speak a lot of languages. I could be very useful to the Church in times like these.'

'Well, if you've got time, you could still see Meggie,' said Anne before she had time to think.

He looked at her with cool, intelligent eyes. He seemed to know what she was thinking. For about ten minutes he said nothing.

'Where is she?' he asked at last in a perfectly normal voice.

'Meggie's in a cottage on Matlock Island. It's a very small place, there are hardly any people there this time of year. If you're going, you'd better pretend to be Luke.'

He gave the sleeping baby back to her. 'Thank you,' he said, going to his car.

◆

Old Rob's car approached along the road to the cottage, stopped and let out a man dressed in shorts and a shirt, with a suitcase in his hand.

'Bye, Mr O'Neill!' Rob shouted as he went.

But Meggie would never again mistake them, Luke O'Neill and Ralph de Bricassart. Even at a distance she knew it was Ralph. She stood silently, waiting for him.

'Hello, Ralph,' she said, not looking at him.

'Hello, Meggie.'

She made him some tea, and they sat drinking it in silence.

'What's the matter, Meggie?' he said at last. She looked at him, and he realized that she saw him as a man, while he still thought of her as a beautiful child. As she looked at him, he saw that she had realized her mistake.

She turned to run out of the cottage, trying to escape from her confused feelings, but he caught her before she got to the door. He held her tightly, and they kissed. Suddenly, his feelings changed, and he realized that this was what he had wanted all these years. He picked her up and carried her to the bed.

◆

For the first time in his life, Ralph woke up in the same bed as another person.

'If I had the energy, I'd go for a swim and then make breakfast,' he said.

'Have your swim. I'll make the breakfast,' she said, smiling at him. 'There's no need to wear any clothes. No one comes here.'

He sat up and stretched. 'It's a beautiful morning.' He stood up, then turned and held out his hand. 'Come with me? We can have breakfast together afterwards.'

The sea was beautiful, the sun was hot, but the wind was cool.

'I feel as if I've never seen the world before,' he said, looking around him.

Meggie took his hand. 'You haven't seen this world before. This is our world, for as long as we're together.'

'What's Luke like?' he asked her later.

'He's like you a bit. He doesn't need women either. You both think that it's weak to need a woman.'

'And you still want us?'

She smiled. 'Oh, Ralph. It's made me so unhappy, but it's the way things are. I can't change you. If I'd really wanted to, I'd have married a good, kind man like my father, someone who did want and need me.'

♦

Day followed day and night followed night. They walked and lay on the beach and swam. He was teaching her to swim. Sometimes he looked sad, knowing that he must go back to the Church.

One day he turned to her, as they lay on the beach.

'Meggie, I've never been so happy, or so unhappy.'

'I know, Ralph.'

'You've always understood me. Is that why I love you?'

'Are you leaving?'

'Tomorrow. I must. My ship leaves in less than a week. I'm going to Rome. For a long time, perhaps even for the rest of my life.'

'Don't worry, Ralph. I'm ready to let you go. I'm leaving Luke, I'm going home to Drogheda.'

They walked and lay on the beach and swam. He was teaching her to swim.

'Oh, my dear! Not because of this, not because of me!'

'No, of course not,' she lied. 'I'd decided before you arrived. Luke doesn't want me or need me, he won't miss me. But I need a home, and I think Drogheda is always going to be home to me. I don't want Justine to grow up in a house where I'm the servant.'

'I'll write to you. Meggie.'

'No, don't. I don't need letters, after this. No one must ever know about this time we've had together.'

He held her close, stroking her hair. 'Meggie, I wish I could marry you. I don't want to leave you. But we can't change what we are. Remember always that I love you.'

The next day Rob appeared and drove Ralph away. Ralph sat in the car and didn't look back. When Rob shook his hand to say goodbye he thought that Ralph's face looked very sad and very human. The expression in his eyes had changed for ever.

◆

When Meggie came back to Himmelhoch, Anne knew at once she would lose her. It was the same Meggie, and yet, in some way, she had changed. When her eyes met Anne's, they were shining with happiness.

'Thank you, Anne.'

'For what?'

'For sending Ralph to me. It meant so much to me! Before Ralph came, I'd decided to stay with Luke, but now I know I have to leave him. I'm going back to Drogheda, and I'm never going to leave it again.'

'We'll miss you, but I'm glad. Luke would only make you more unhappy.'

'Do you know where he is?'

'Yes, he's come back from Sydney. He's cutting cane near Ingham.'

'I'll have to go and see him. I've got to tell him, and although I hate the idea, I've got to sleep with him.'

'*What?*'

Meggie's eyes shone. 'I think I'm going to have a baby.'

Anne stared at Meggie, shocked. 'What a mess!' she said.

'But Anne, don't you understand? I could never have Ralph. I've always known that. But now I've got part of him. I've always loved Ralph, but he'll never be mine, he belongs to the Church. But his son – I know the baby's going to be a son – will belong to me.'

'Oh, Meggie,' Anne said helplessly.

◆

As Meggie took the little train to Ingham, she thought that she was ready to do anything for Ralph's baby, even sleep with Luke.

When she arrived at the little town she went to the cleanest looking hotel and found a telephone. She left a message at the farm where Luke was working, then went back to her room to wait. She took her clothes off and sat on the bed, nervous and shaking.

At nine o'clock Luke arrived. He knocked on the door of her room and she opened it slowly without speaking. Luke thought she looked beautiful. He reached out, picked her up and carried her to the bed.

Meggie didn't speak to Luke all night, although her touch had been very welcoming. In the morning she moved away from him.

'What brings you to Ingham, Meg?' he asked.

Her head turned and she stared at him coldly.

'I came to tell you I'm going home to Drogheda,' she said.

For a moment he didn't believe her, then he saw the expression on her face.

'But why?'

'You're a fool, Luke,' she said. 'You've treated your wife and daughter like dogs. You've got twenty thousand pounds in the bank, and you won't even take me to Sydney with you!'

'Oh, Meg!' he said, astonished. 'I've never been cruel to you. You've had enough to eat, somewhere to live —'

'Oh, yes,' she interrupted. 'It's useless talking to you. It's like talking to the wall. You can keep the money in the bank, Luke. But you're not going to get any more money from me. I'll need it for Justine, and for the new baby if I'm lucky!'

'So that's why you came,' he said. 'You wanted another baby, not me.'

'That's right,' she said. 'And I never want to see you again.'

After she had left, Luke sat and stared at the closed door for a long time. Then he got up and started to dress. If he hurried he could get a ride back to the farm with his friends.

FIVE:

1938–1953 FEE

Chapter Fourteen

And so Meggie returned to the brown and silver land around Drogheda. As she drove from Gillanbone, clouds of dust rose into the air and the silver-grey grass stretched towards the sky.

Then she saw the big house, and the gardens full of flowers, and Mrs Smith, the housekeeper, standing outside the house, her mouth open in surprise. The other servants ran out, laughing and crying. Meggie was home.

Fee came out to see what all the noise was about.

'Hello, Mum. I've come home.'

And although Fee's expression didn't change, Meggie knew that her mother was glad to see her.

'Have you left Luke?' Fee asked.

'Yes, I shall never go back to him. He didn't want a home, or his children, or me.'

'Children?'

'Yes, I'm going to have another baby.'

Meggie moved back into her old room, with Justine in the room next to it. Bob was glad to see her, too. Jack and Hughie greeted her, smiling shyly. The twins, Jims and Patsy, had grown up and left school. They were working at Drogheda, too.

'I've never seen it so dry, Meggie,' Bob said. 'There's been no rain for two years.'

'Can I help?' she asked.

'Of course! Can you do the same job as before?'

Meggie went back to work. It felt good to be riding her horse across the fields, watching the birds and the sky.

♦

Meggie's son was born on the first of October. He was a beautiful baby, with Ralph's eyes.

Fee stared at the baby. 'Have you decided on his name?' she asked.

'I'm going to call him Dane.'

Meggie looked down at the baby she loved so much. He is enough to make me happy, she thought. And Ralph de Bricassart will never know what she had stolen from him. She would never tell him the truth about Dane. Ralph was far away in Rome – he would never know he had a son.

Chapter Fifteen

The radio brought the news to Drogheda that the war in Europe had come at last. Germany had attacked Poland and now the Australian government needed men to fight.

Jims and Patsy planned to join the army when they were old enough, and Meggie said that she would again help to run the farm when they went. A year later, the twins left on the train for Sydney and by the beginning of 1941 they were in Egypt. In Queensland, Luke continued cutting sugar cane.

There was still no rain at Drogheda, and they had to buy food to feed the sheep. Meggie often worked seven days a week because Bob needed her help.

Dane was a beautiful child. Nobody except Meggie seemed to notice how much he looked like Ralph. He had the same eyes, the same face; only one thing, his golden hair, was different. Justine loved her little brother, and the two children went everywhere together.

'Don't worry, Mum,' Justine said. 'I'll look after Dane for you.' These days, Justine was smiling and laughing – she laughed when Dane laughed, and Dane was always laughing. Meggie was full of regret that she had to work so hard, and miss her children growing up.

The war continued. Jims and Patsy fought in North Africa, then arrived home in Australia to get ready to fight the Japanese. When they visited Drogheda they were grown up, taller and stronger, their faces serious and silent. They loved Dane and played with him for hours.

'Don't ever let him leave Drogheda, Meggie,' said Jims. 'On Drogheda he can't come to any harm.'

Chapter Sixteen

On the same day that the war ended, on September 2, 1945, the rain at last came to Gillanbone. Hardly any rain had fallen for ten years, but now twelve inches of rain fell on the thirsty earth.

After the rain, green grass began to grow. Bob, Jack, Hughie and Patsy went back to work. Jims was still recovering from a wound he had received while fighting the Japanese. Meggie realized that soon Jims would be home, other men would be free to work at Drogheda, and she would be able to spend more time with the children.

She received a letter from Luke.

'How's Luke?' Fee asked.

'Just the same, Mum. He's still talking about a few more years cutting sugar. Then he'll buy a farm.'

'Will he?'

'I suppose so, one day.'

'Would you go to join him, Meggie?'

'No, never.'

Fee sat down in a chair beside her daughter. 'You could marry again, you know,' she said. 'There are plenty of men around here who are interested in you.'

'It's against the laws of the Church. And I don't want to marry again. I'm happy here with my children. They're so different, Dane and Justine, but they get along so well together,' said Meggie. 'It's surprising – they never fight.'

Fee was watching Dane. 'He looks so like his father,' she said, as the boy disappeared from sight.

Meggie felt suddenly cold, then realized that Fee meant, of course, that Dane looked like Luke.

'Do you think so, Mum?' she asked. 'I can never see it myself. Dane is really nothing like Luke.'

Fee laughed, and her eyes looked into Meggie's face. 'I'm not a fool, Meggie. I don't mean Luke O'Neill. I mean Dane looks exactly like Ralph de Bricassart.'

Meggie felt as if her heart had stopped.

'Mum,' she said, hardly able to speak. 'What a strange thing to say! Father Ralph de Bricassart!'

'Of course,' said Fee. 'I knew it as soon as Dane was born.'

'Well, it isn't true!' said Meggie angrily.

Suddenly, Fee put her hand on Meggie's knee and smiled. 'Don't lie to me, Meggie. I'm not a fool, I've got eyes.'

Meggie sighed. 'Is it obvious, Mum? Does everybody know?'

'Of course not,' said Fee. 'I know because I've been watching you and Ralph de Bricassart for years. He was a stubborn man, he wanted to be a perfect priest; you always came second to that. But it wasn't any good, was it? Something happened in the end. He was jealous when you married Luke. I could see it when I told him about it. I knew that something had happened when you came back to Drogheda. Once you had Ralph de Bricassart it wasn't necessary to stay with Luke.'

'Yes,' sighed Meggie. 'Ralph found me at last. It didn't help us much, except that I've got his child now.'

Fee laughed. 'I felt like that once.'

'Frank?'

Fee stood up. 'Oh, you know about that, do you? I couldn't have Frank's father, he was married already. He was one of the most important men in New Zealand. I loved him so much, I thought I would go mad with love for him.'

'So that's why you loved Frank more than the rest of us,' Meggie said.

'I thought I did, because of his father. I've never been happy since the day I met that man. And then Frank . . . I ignored the rest of the family because I loved Frank so much. I ignored Paddy, who was so good to me, but I couldn't see it. Meggie, it's wrong to love like that. It's a mistake. I made that mistake, and you're making it, too. I lost Frank, and one day you'll lose Dane.'

'No, I won't,' said Meggie angrily. 'I'll keep him safe, here on Drogheda.'

'Paddy wasn't safe here, neither was Stu. Nowhere is safe.

70

You can't keep Dane here if he wants to go. You couldn't hold the father, how can you hold his son?'

'If you tell Dane about his father, Mum, I'll kill you!'

'Don't worry. I won't say anything. Your secret's safe.'

◆

The rain came and went, and gradually the land recovered. The number of sheep increased, and Drogheda made more and more money. Life was suddenly very pleasant. Dane and Justine were growing up. When Dane was ten and Justine eleven they were sent to school in Sydney.

A Sydney newspaper of August 4, 1952 had an interesting piece about Ralph de Bricassart. He was now a cardinal in Rome.

'I wonder if he remembers us?' Meggie sighed.

'Of course. He still looks after Mary Carson's money. He still pays us for looking after Drogheda. How could he forget?'

'That's true. And we've made a lot of money for his Church, haven't we?'

'What will you do if he comes back, Meggie?'

'He'll never come here again!'

'He might,' said Fee.

He did, in December. No one even knew he was in Australia. No one heard him arrive as his car stopped outside the big house. It was summer and there were roses, like the one Meggie had once given him. He heard a laugh from behind one of the rose trees. It was a childish laugh, like Meggie's. He looked through the branches.

But Meggie wasn't there, only a boy sitting on the grass and playing a game with a small pig. Cardinal Ralph stepped forward. The boy, aged about twelve or fourteen, looked up, surprised. The pig ran away.

'Hello,' said the boy, smiling.

'Hello,' said Cardinal Ralph. 'Who are you?'

'I'm Dane O'Neill,' answered the boy. 'Who are you?'

'My name is Ralph de Bricassart.'

'May I help you?' the boy asked, standing up.

'Is your father here, Dane?'

'*My father?*' The boy frowned. 'No, he's never been here.'

'Oh, I see. Is your mother here, then?'

'She's in Gillanbone, but she'll be back soon. Would you like to speak to my grandmother? She's in the house.' Then the boy stared at him. 'Ralph de Bricassart! You're Cardinal de Bricassart! I'm sorry. I didn't mean to be rude!'

'It's all right, Dane. I'm here as a friend of your mother's and your grandmother's.'

Suddenly they were interrupted by Justine. Cardinal Ralph recognized her red hair and light blue eyes. She didn't seem to be impressed by the Cardinal.

'May I go and look for your grandmother?' he asked.

'Of course. Do you need us?' Justine asked.

'No, thank you. I know the way.' Cardinal Ralph moved off towards the house. He found Fee working at her desk.

'Hello, Fee,' he said.

'Hello, Ralph,' she answered calmly. 'How nice to see you. I didn't know you were in Australia.'

'I'm just having a few weeks' holiday. I wanted to see Drogheda again.'

Cardinal Ralph left Fee to her work and walked down towards the river. He remembered all the buildings, all the familiar flowers and trees. Then he turned and saw Meggie walking towards him. She was still as beautiful as he remembered her.

She came closer, then her arms were around his neck.

'Meggie, Meggie,' he said, his face in her hair.

'It doesn't seem to matter, does it?' she said. 'Nothing changes.'

'I'm Dane O'Neill,' answered the boy. 'Who are you?'

'No, nothing changes,' he said.

'This is Drogheda,' she said. 'When you're here, you're mine, not God's.'

'I know. But I still had to come.' He pulled her down beside him on the grass. 'Why did you do it, Meggie?'

'Do what?'

'Why did you go back to Luke? Why did you have his son?' he asked jealously.

'He made me do it. It was only once,' she said without expression. 'But I had Dane, so I'm not sorry it happened.'

'I'm sorry,' he said. 'I shouldn't have asked. He's a wonderful boy. Does he look like Luke?'

She smiled secretly. 'Not really. Neither of the children look like Luke, or me.'

'I love them because they're yours.'

'What do you think of Dane?' she asked eagerly.

'I liked him. His laugh sounds like yours.'

♦

It was Saturday night, and Bob, Jack, Hughie, Jims and Patsy were in for dinner. After the meal, when Dane and Justine had gone to bed, Cardinal Ralph called all the family together.

'I've got something to tell you,' he said. 'It's about Frank.'

For a moment they were all silent, then Fee spoke.

'What about Frank?' she asked calmly.

'Frank has served thirty years in prison,' said the Cardinal. 'I know my people here have given you news of Frank, but they haven't given you the bad news. I didn't want you to know about Frank's loneliness and hopelessness, because there was nothing any of us could do about it. Frank was very violent at first, that's why he's been in prison so long.'

Fee looked up quickly. 'It's his temper,' she said.

The Cardinal continued. 'You must be wondering why I

came here after all these years,' he said, without looking at Meggie. 'Well, I came back to see what I could do about Frank.'

They all stared at him and waited.

'Frank is going to be set free,' said the Cardinal.

'Thank you,' said Fee.

'He isn't the same Frank,' Ralph continued. 'I visited him in prison before I came here. I told him you all knew he was in prison. He's so quiet now, he was simply grateful when I told him. And he's looking forward to seeing you all again, especially you, Fee.'

'When's he coming?' asked Bob.

'In a week or two. He wants to come by train.'

'I'll meet him,' said Fee. 'On my own. And now,' she said, going back to her desk. 'I have work to do.'

The five brothers went to bed, followed by Meggie. Fee continued to sit at her desk, thinking.

Ralph climbed the stairs. At the top, the house was silent, but Meggie's door was open, waiting for him. He shut the door behind him, then locked it.

'Were you sure I'd come to you, Meggie?' he asked.

'I told you. On Drogheda you're mine,' She went across to the lamp, and turned it out.

◆

Dane was disappointed. 'I thought you'd wear red,' he said to the Cardinal.

'I do, sometimes, but only in the palace.'

'Do you really have a palace?'

'Yes.'

'I'd love to see it.'

Cardinal Ralph smiled. 'Who knows, Dane? Perhaps one day you will.'

◆

Luddie and Anne Mueller were coming to Drogheda for Christmas, and everyone there was looking forward to the best Christmas in years.

Meggie was happy, having both Dane and Ralph near her. One thing disturbed her happiness; Ralph hadn't realized that Dane was his son. She didn't intend to tell him. If he couldn't see for himself, why should she tell him?

The phone rang. It was for Fee. She took the phone, listening, and, said, 'Thank you.'

'What is it, Mum?' Meggie asked.

'Frank's out of prison. He's arriving this afternoon.' She looked at her watch. 'I must leave soon.'

'Isn't it wonderful, Mum? Frank's coming home in time for Christmas!'

'Yes,' said Fee, almost sadly. 'It's wonderful.'

◆

Fee stood alone on the station platform, waiting for Frank's train.

When it arrived, Frank stood there as if he didn't know what to do next. He was fifty-two years old now, a middle-aged man. He was thin, and his clothes hung loosely. He seemed not to expect anyone to meet him.

Fee walked towards him.

'Hello, Frank,' she said.

His eyes, which used to shine, now looked dull. He raised them to his mother's face. He looked exhausted and patient. As he looked at his mother he had a strange, wounded expression in his eyes, like a dying man.

'Oh, Frank!' she said, and took him in her arms, his head on her shoulder. 'It's all right, it's all right.'

Frank sat silently in the car as they drove back to Drogheda. He looked out of the window as they left the town.

'It looks exactly the same,' he whispered. 'I never thought I'd see it again.'

When they were approaching the house he sighed. 'I'd forgotten how lovely it is here,' he said softly.

◆

Fee did all she could to help Frank to fit into life at Drogheda. She knew he would never be like the old Frank; he'd lost his old energy and enthusiasm for life. His brothers didn't want him to work with them, and he had never, even in the old days, enjoyed their work. But he loved the gardens, and gradually he found work for himself there.

But Fee wasn't entirely happy. Seeing Frank often made her sad, he was so changed. He was a ruined man, who had suffered things she couldn't imagine.

One day after Frank had been home for six months, Meggie came into the room to see her mother watching Frank as he worked in the garden. The expression on Fee's face made Meggie's heart sink.

'Oh, Mum!' she said helplessly.

Fee looked at her, shook her head and smiled. 'It doesn't matter, Meggie,' she said.

'I wish I could do something!'

'You can. Just stay here. I'm very grateful to you. You help me a lot.'

SIX:
1954–1965 DANE

Chapter Seventeen

To Meggie's surprise, Justine decided to become an actress. Soon

Dane would have to decide. Meggie had always hoped and expected that he would come back to Drogheda and work with his uncles.

One day, as they sat alone together in the garden, Dane spoke to Meggie about his future.

'I'm going to be a priest,' he said. 'I want to offer myself to God. It won't be easy, but I'm going to do it.'

Dane couldn't understand the look in Meggie's eyes. Instead of being pleased, she looked as if she was going to die.

'Oh, Mum, can't you understand?' he said. 'I've never wanted to be anything but a priest! I can't be anything else!'

Meggie recovered at last. 'You gave me a shock,' she said. 'Of course I'm glad for you. I didn't expect this, that's all.'

'You're sure you don't mind?'

'Of course not,' she lied. 'What are you planning to do about it?'

'I thought I'd train to be a priest in Sydney,' he said.

Meggie thought about this. 'I've got a better idea,' she said at last. 'I shall send you to Rome, to Cardinal de Bricassart. He'll look after you.'

Meggie walked slowly back to the house.

'What is it, Meggie?' Fee asked.

Meggie sat down. 'You were right. You said I'd lose Dane. I didn't believe you, but it's happened.'

'How have you lost him?'

'He's going to be a priest.' She began to laugh and cry at the same time. 'I stole Ralph from God, and now God is taking my son away from me. I'm paying for what I did.'

'Is Dane going to Sydney?' Fee asked.

'No, that wouldn't be paying enough, would it? I'm going to send him to Ralph in Rome. Let Ralph have him at last.'

'Are you going to tell Ralph about Dane?'

'No, and he'll never guess,' said Meggie. 'I'm sending him my son, not his.'

'Be careful, Meggie.'

'What else can happen to me now?' she asked.

◆

Cardinal Ralph remembered Meggie's letter as he looked at the boy.

'I pass the responsibility for Dane to you,' she wrote. 'What I stole, I give back. Promise that if he stops wanting to be a priest, you'll send him back to me. He belonged to me first.'

'Dane, are you sure?' he asked.

'Absolutely.'

'What would you do if you ever changed your mind?'

'Why, I'd ask to leave,' said Dane, surprised.

Cardinal Ralph sighed. 'Why did you want to come to me, Dane?'

'Because I always think of you as being the perfect priest.'

Cardinal Ralph frowned. 'No, Dane, I'm far from perfect. I've broken the laws of the Church.'

'I understand that it takes a long time to become a perfect priest. It must involve great pain and suffering.'

◆

Justine left Sydney and moved to London to work as an actress. When the summer came she travelled to Rome to see Dane. When he met her on the station platform he looked the same Dane, but he was different. He was part of a different world.

'I have two months holiday, Jussy,' he said. 'We can see France and Spain and still have time to go back to Drogheda. I miss the old place.'

'Do you?' she said. 'I don't miss it at all; London's far too interesting.'

Chapter Eighteen

It took Dane eight years in Rome to become a priest. The Drogheda people planned a trip to Rome, to see the ceremony when Dane became a priest.

'I'm not going to Rome!' said Meggie firmly to Anne Mueller. 'I'm never going to leave Drogheda again.'

'Meggie, don't! You can't disappoint Dane! Go, please!'

'Go to Rome and see the smile on Ralph de Bricassart's face? I'd rather be dead!'

'Oh, Meggie, Meggie!' said Anne. 'Why don't you forget about your pride and go to Rome? You're only hurting Ralph, and your son.'

'It isn't pride, it's fear,' said Meggie. 'I feel that if I go to Rome something terrible will happen.'

'Nonsense, Meggie. Why don't you just get on that plane and go?'

'Oh, leave me alone!' said Meggie angrily.

♦

Justine and her uncles, dressed in their unfamiliar black suits, watched the ceremony as Dane became a priest. Cardinal Ralph watched too, tears in his eyes. Dane would be a fine priest, a better priest than the Cardinal. He wondered why Meggie hadn't come – it was a great gift she had given to God.

Afterwards, Dane spoke to Justine first. He had missed his mother at the ceremony.

'Father O'Neill,' she said.

'I can't believe it yet, Jus.'

After a while he said, 'I'm so pleased Frank came. I feel so sorry for him sometimes.'

Justine ignored this. 'I could kill Mum!' she said. 'Why did she do this to you?'

'I don't believe she meant to hurt me,' he said. 'I've got to see her, though, and find out what the matter is. But first I'd like to go to Greece for two weeks. Will you go with me?'

'Oh, Dane, of course I'll go.'

◆

But when Justine woke up the next morning there was a letter waiting for her. It was from a producer in London, offering her work in a play. It was a wonderful opportunity.

She realized that now she wouldn't be able to go to Greece with Dane. But Dane would understand, he always did.

◆

So Dane went to Greece alone. In Athens the atmosphere was tense; people talked about a revolution. He took a ferry to Crete. Here he found a peaceful place to stay among the mountains. He spent his days walking and praying. It was hot, and quiet, and very sleepy.

Dane had never been so happy. He felt close to God, and ready to begin his life as a priest.

He walked one day to a little beach where he liked to swim. There were two young men on one end of the beach, and two young women, speaking German, on the other. They stopped talking and smiled at him. He greeted the young men.

'Be careful,' one of them said. 'The sea's dangerous today. There must be a storm somewhere. It's too strong for us.'

'Thanks,' Dane smiled, and ran into the sea.

The sea seemed to be calm, but it pulled strongly at his legs, trying to drag him under. But he was too strong a swimmer to be worried by it. He swam smoothly across the little bay. When he stopped and looked around he noticed that the two German women were running, laughing, into the waves.

He shouted to them to stay in the shallow water. They laughed and waved at him. He put his head down and swam again. Then he thought he heard a cry. He looked again and saw the women struggling in the water. He could hear them screaming.

He swam rapidly towards them. Their arms reached out to him, dragging him under. Coughing, he managed to grab hold of them and began pulling them towards the shore.

As he approached the shore, the two men reached out to help him. His toes touched the sand; he was exhausted as he pushed the women to safety. While he rested, the sea reached out and dragged him back again.

Then he was seized by a terrible pain in his chest. My heart! he thought. I don't want to die! Not yet, not before I've begun my work!

He turned on his back and stared up at the sky. I must accept the pain, he thought. It's what God wants from me. His body shook, then it was still.

Back on the beach, the two men pulled the women up onto the sand and looked out to sea. But the bay was empty. Dane was gone.

An hour later, a helicopter found his body out at sea, floating on the waves. At first they thought he was still alive, but then they realized he was dead.

◆

Justine's phone rang at nine in the morning. She picked it up sleepily.

'Hello?'

'Miss Justine O'Neill? Do you have a brother, Mr Dane O'Neill?'

'Yes, I do.'

'I'm sorry, Miss O'Neill, I've got some bad news for you. I regret that Mr O'Neill was drowned yesterday in Crete.'

Justine couldn't speak. She could hardly breathe.

'Miss O'Neill, are you there, Miss O'Neill?'

'Yes, yes.'

'I understand you're his closest relation. We need to know what to do about the body. Are you there, Miss O'Neill?'

'You'll have to ask my mother . . .'

Justine gave the speaker Meggie's address in Australia, then sat down on the floor beside the telephone. She couldn't believe that Dane was dead. How could he have drowned? Why hadn't she been there to protect him?

Then she thought about her mother, and knew that Meggie mustn't hear the news from a stranger. She must phone Drogheda immediately.

◆

Meggie answered the phone herself. It was late, and Fee had gone to bed.

'Mum? Is that you, Mum?'

'Yes, it's Mum here,' said Meggie gently, realizing that Justine was upset.

Justine was crying now. 'Mum, Dane's dead. Dane's dead!'

Meggie felt as if she was sinking into a deep, dark hole with no bottom. This was it, the worst thing that could happen.

'Keep calm, Justine,' she said. 'Where did it happen? In Rome? What about the Cardinal?'

'It happened in Greece. The Cardinal probably doesn't know anything about it.'

Meggie tried to comfort Justine. 'Don't cry. We'll bring Dane home to Drogheda. I'll phone and make arrangements. He belongs here. Come with him, Justine.'

But with the revolution in Greece, arrangements were hard to make. Meggie and the family waited in Drogheda, but nothing happened. Then Justine, in London, got a message. They had buried Dane in Greece, and no one seemed to know where.

So Meggie decided to go to Rome.

'I'm going to see Ralph de Bricassart,' she told the family. 'If anyone can help us, he can.'

◆

Cardinal Ralph hardly knew Meggie when she came into the room. She was fifty-three now and he was seventy-one. They hadn't met for thirteen years. The sweetness had left her face and she refused to look into his eyes.

'Is anything the matter?' he asked anxiously.

Then she lifted her eyes and looked at him steadily. There was something awful in those eyes.

'Dane is dead,' said Meggie.

He put his hands over his face. He couldn't believe that Dane, the perfect young priest, was dead.

'I came to ask for your help,' said Meggie quickly. 'I don't really care how you feel about Dane.'

The Cardinal's face was full of suffering. 'How can I help, Meggie?' he asked quietly.

'I want my boy back, Ralph. I want him found and brought back to Drogheda.'

'Of course,' he said gently. 'I've got friends in Greece. I'm sure they'll help to arrange it.'

'You don't understand, Ralph. I want you to go to Greece yourself, with me, now.'

'But Meggie, I can't leave Rome at the moment. I've got work to do here. Very important work.'

She reached a decision. 'What would you do if he were your own son, Ralph?' she asked. 'Dane *was* your son.'

'What?' he asked, staring at her.

'I never meant to tell you,' she said, looking at him without pity. 'But now he doesn't belong to either of us. He belongs to God.'

◆

'I came to ask for your help,' said Meggie quickly.

And so they brought Dane back to Drogheda and buried him there. After the ceremony Cardinal Ralph looked at Meggie once, and then couldn't look into her face again. Justine caught the afternoon plane back to Sydney, and her uncles, tired after a long day, went early to bed. The Cardinal sat, thinking of Dane, thinking of Meggie. Meggie and Fee sat opposite him, side by side.

Suddenly, there was a mist in front of Ralph's eyes. Meggie and Fee were speaking, but he couldn't hear them. They were coming towards him, but he couldn't see them properly. He hardly felt the pain, only felt Meggie's arms around him for the last time. He managed to turn his eyes and look at her. He wanted to say, Forgive me, and saw that she had forgiven him long ago. So he closed his eyes, and felt, for the last time, forgetfulness in Meggie.

EXERCISES

Vocabulary Work

Look back at the 'Dictionary Words' in this book. Check that you understand them all. Write sentences using *two or more* of these words in each sentence, showing their meanings clearly.

Comprehension

Chapters 1–4

1 Who are these people?
  a He was the only Cleary child with black hair.
  b She gave Father Ralph a new car.
  c She was so ill on the trip from New Zealand to Australia that the others thought she would die.

Chapters 5–8

2 Answer these questions:
  a How does Frank win twenty pounds?
  b What does Paddy make known during his argument with Frank?
  c Mary Carson says that she hates her life and would like to destroy Ralph's. Why does she feel this way?
  d What does Fee discover when she is wrapping her cups in old newspapers, ready to move to the big house?

Chapters 9–13

3 Are these sentences true (√) or not true (x)?
  a Jack finds Paddy's dead body after the fire.
  b Meggie and Luke O'Neill are married in Gillanbone and then go on a train journey to North Queensland.
  c The first summer Meggie is at Himmelhoch, Luke goes to Sydney and takes her with him.

87

4 Put these sentences in the right order:

a Cardinal Ralph hardly knew Meggie when she came into the room. She was fifty-three now and he was seventy-one.

b The radio brought news to Drogheda that the war in Europe had come at last.

c Dane had never been so happy. He felt close to God and ready to begin his life as a priest.

d Fee stood alone on the station platform, waiting for Frank's train.

Discussion

1 What would have happened if:

a Ralph had destroyed Mary Carson's will?

b Luke hadn't gone to work at Drogheda?

2 Which of these characters behaved best? Which behaved worst?

Fee   Meggie   Mary Carson   Ralph   Luke

Writing

1 Imagine one of the characters in the story is writing for advice to a problem page in a magazine. Write his or her letter and an answer giving your advice (about 150 words).

2 Look back at all the pictures of Meggie. Now write two or three sentences describing Meggie: as a small child, a young woman and a middle–aged woman.

Review

1 Are the people in the story to blame for the bad things that happen to them, or do they have bad luck?

2 If you were making a film of *The Thorn Birds*, which would be the best scene? Why?

The Sheffield College

PARSON CROSS CENTRE
Library/Learning Centre